'I'm a very physical man.'

'I'm afraid...afraid of loving you...afraid of losing you. See, you shouldn't be interested in me at all.'

'Little one, hush!' James put his arms around her, enfolding her. 'It's natural to be afraid. Someone has damaged your self-esteem. That affects your ability to receive love as well as give love. I want to help, Ally, but you have to trust me enough to tell me.'

Dear Reader

The summer holidays are now behind us—but Mills & Boon still have lots of treats in store for you! Why not indulge yourself in long, romantic evenings by the fire? We're sure you'll find our heroes simply irresistible! And perhaps you'd like to experience the exotic beauty of the Bahamas—or the glamour of Milan? Whatever you fancy, just curl up with this month's selection of enchanting love stories—and let your favourite authors carry you away!

Happy reading!

The Editor

Rosalie Henaghan grew up on the family farm in New Zealand. As a child, she saw nothing exotic in feeding cattle, mustering sheep, checking stock or tramping in the bush. Trained as a teacher, Rosalie entered radio, where she had her own daily programme. Writing and editing scripts developed her storytelling ability and, interviewing author Essie Summers, Rosalie received encouragement to 'sit down and write...'

COLOURS OF LOVE

BY
ROSALIE HENAGHAN

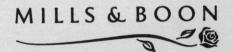

MILLS & BOON

MILLS & BOON LIMITED
ETON HOUSE, 18-24 PARADISE ROAD
RICHMOND, SURREY TW9 1SR

*First published in Great Britain 1993
by Mills & Boon Limited*

© Rosalie Henaghan 1993

*Australian copyright 1993
Philippine copyright 1993
This edition 1993*

ISBN 0 263 78286 7

*Set in Times Roman 10 on 11¼ pt.
01-9311-58606 C*

Made and printed in Great Britain

CHAPTER ONE

'ALLY—Alice, new shoes!'

Ally Barrett smiled at the triumphant toddler, then scooped up Geoffrey's twin and sat her on the bench. 'Greer, your turn!' With deft fingers she removed her small charge's trainers and turned to look for the shop assistant, who had gone to the rear to fetch a second pair of shoes.

'Good morning, madam. I regret your assistant has been delayed. I understand you require these shoes.'

The man nestled a pair of tiny black shoes in his large hand. In the other hand he carried three small shoe-boxes. He smiled at the brown-haired twins, and their eyes widened as they gazed up and up and up at the newcomer. Ally understood their wonder. The man who stood in front of them was six feet tall with a rugged, athletic body which spoke more of playing-fields than executive offices, although his suit in a fine grey wool exemplified tailoring perfection. Ally noted that his simple white shirt was cuffed with gold links, but was reassured by the regulation burgundy tie, patterned with the small cursive T design, of all Tasman's department store male staff.

She felt an instinctive rush of appreciation, then scorned her facile emotions as she realised that the man's ski-bronzed skin had crinkled into humour lines around his blue eyes. The man knew he was good-looking and revelled in female homage! The trendy haircut, the clothes, all bespoke self-interest. He was Establishment, she surmised, a man who rated money as success, giving away little, unless connected with his own advancement. As he sized up Greer's dainty feet, the man's eyes met her own brown-eyed glance in the mirror, and she had the impression that they exchanged thoughts, startling each other. She had been dismissing him, but he had been equally disapproving of her!

Unsettled, Ally turned to Geoffrey, who smiled lovingly at her, and her good mood returned. What did she care what the Establishment Adonis thought? Lifting a hand to her hair, she checked that the cascade of narrow carmine ribbons still looped and braided her flyaway mane of long gold curls into place. She liked her outfit; the troubadour coat with its sweeping lily sleeves and swirling jewel colours of carmine, olive and sapphire had been a patchwork triumph; under the coat she wore a long-line, sloppy sweatshirt and tights in the same olive. It was warm and practical for her work as a nanny and it pleased her own sense of colour and fantasy.

'Ally, Ally—Alice! Raisins, please,' crooned Geoffrey as he edged himself down from the bench.

'I'll get them, Geoffrey.' She repositioned him and reached into her patchwork carryall, putting it beside her on the seat. She looked at Greer to see if she wanted some raisins too, and intercepted the look of amused distaste on the sensuously carved lips of the assistant. The man was looking at her bag, and her mood evaporated as she saw her carryall through his eyes. It did look grubby, but she wasn't going to explain to any supercilious, conceited, suit-wearing male that Geoffrey had thrown it overboard from the pushchair and, with typical targeting, it had landed in a wet clay-pile where the street was being dug up. She had wiped the muck from it, but the rich red, olive and sapphire-blue patches had been stained. If she could have managed without it, she would have returned it to the car, but the twins needed many items on expeditions, whether spare pants, tissues, drinks, raisins or toys. Seizing the carryall, she thrust it out of sight under the bench. To her dismay, a thick streak of ochre muddied the otherwise immaculate burgundy buttoned leather seating. It didn't take much imagination to realise the assistant would think Geoffrey had disgraced himself. She could picture the shrug of the assistant, the heaven-raised eyes and the silent 'Typical!'

Against the restrained elegance and subdued décor of the shoe section of Tasman's, the city's leading department store, she was as out of place as a rock video at a funeral. She felt uncomfortable in the upmarket surroundings, silver-grey walls with their single narrow burgundy stripe, the fittings superbly polished rosewood and brass period pieces. If the twins' mother had not told her to buy the shoes at Tasman's where she could use the account, she would have taken them to another shop where toddlers' needs had been considered. And with pleasant staff!

Ally realised she was being sour; the first assistant had been knowledgeable and kind, and Greer was behaving with angelic courtesy, smiling up at the man with instinctive pleasure, fluttering her eyelashes as he measured her feet. It was only when Greer saw the black shoes that trouble loomed.

'Want red shoes!' Greer's jaw jutted. 'Like Ally's!'

Ally saw the man's glance flick to her own red boots and follow the line of her legs up to her buttocks, and too late she realised her sweatshirt had ruched up when she had swung Greer on to the seat. An appreciative smile played on his handsome face. Ally tugged down her top and glared at him. She drew in a breath as his blue eyes challenged her, daring her to look at him, as with slow, relaxed movements he rose to his male-dominating height.

Rainbows of attraction shimmered between them. Stunned, Ally picked up Geoffrey as a defence mechanism. Her brows drew together as she tried to compose herself, deciding she must have fantasised the surge of sensuality. The man was good-looking, but... She glanced at the assistant. It hadn't been her imagination. His smile was whipped cream and apple pie, as he waited for instructions.

'Ally, red shoes, please!'

Greer, eyes big with hope. Sanity returned with the child's words. Geoffrey wriggled to get down and she released him, considering Greer's request. The children's mother had said nothing about colour, and red shoes would work with Greer's wardrobe. 'Do you have some similar in red?' she asked.

When he moved away to fetch the shoes she expelled a long, gusty breath she hadn't even known she had been holding. The sight of the streak of clay on the burgundy seat reminded her, and she took out some tissues to remove the mark. She checked the twins. Geoffrey was amusing himself with the shoe display behind him and Greer was dancing, entranced with her 'town dress' self in the mirror. Ally wiped away the clay, then located the gleaming brass rubbish tin beside the counter and deposited the tissues. Walking back from the counter, she was appalled to see that Geoffrey had climbed down and was toddling at full speed towards the escalator. The returning assistant had realised the danger and they both swooped to the child.

'Madam, escalators can be dangerous!'

'Tell Tasman's that! They're asking for trouble having the children's shoe section right beside it!' Anger and fright snapped in her voice. The sudden proximity with the man had caused a spark-like reaction which exploded through her. From the look on the man's face he had been just as aware of the physical attraction, and when he turned back to the counter, he was deliberately distancing himself. Ally's immediate reaction was to leave, but reason told her that walking out would place a ridiculous emphasis on the incident. It would be unprofessional and unfair to walk out with shoes for Geoffrey and not for Greer. Leading Geoffrey back to the pushchair, she strapped him in, ignoring his loud protests. She looked round to check on Greer and saw her lying on the seat, her attention riveted on pulling off one of the buttons on the bench. 'Greer, no!' She sat her charge upright and distracted her with the red shoes, but let the attendant fit them as Geoffrey was bellowing like a bull on discovering he had been penned. Ally remembered she still had the small packs of raisins. 'Geoffrey, some raisins?'

His yells stopped in the middle of a rising note and he switched on a smile. 'Please, Ally!'

She handed a packet to the eager boy and reserved the second for Greer. Kneeling in front of the little girl, the assistant looked like the prince from *Cinderella* in the book of fairy-tales. His fingers were dexterous as he slipped the shoes into position. Greer stood up, smile marigold-bright.

'Look, Ally!' She danced around, her movements comical as she was bending to admire her new shoes and pirouetting at the same time. 'Red shoes!'

The assistant stood up. 'An excellent fit. Your daughter, like her mother, appreciates colour.'

Ally was about to say that Greer wasn't her daughter, but her sensitivity suspected a derogatory tinge in his voice. 'Colour is fun!' She smiled with saccharine sweetness. 'There are more than enough grey people around!' She bent to check the shoes, but the fit was perfect. 'Do you want to wear them, Greer?' she asked. When the child nodded ecstatically, Ally stood up. At last they could leave!

'Very well, madam, I'll box these for you. Cash or charge?'

He had the old trainers wrapped and was tapping out the details as Ally handed over the card. She glanced at the details of the shoes, including the price, on the end of the box, and her hand froze. She hadn't known a child's shoes could be so expensive. Why hadn't she asked the cost? 'Wait! That's the price?' She saw his surprise at her query. 'That's more than I pay for mine!'

'Madam, size does not necessarily equate with quality.'

Ally bristled at the remark.

'The toddlers' shoes are the best,' he continued. 'They're not expensive, not if you consider the top-grade leather and the excellent workmanship. Superb examples from our export range.'

Greer was preening, examining each red shoe-covered foot in the full-length mirror, her delight obvious. Ally felt sick with dismay. Greer was such a happy, sunshine child and so rarely asked for anything. But when she made up her mind, she could make a howling, moon-intoxicated banshee sound like a singer humming a lullaby. Ally sighed. The whole experience had been a series of disasters from the time the wretched man had taken over. She decided not to be intimidated. Wasn't he supposed to be there to assist her! 'Sorry. Have you another red pair? The same size but a lesser price?'

'Of course, madam.' He pointed to the other two boxes he had brought out, twisting the ends so she could see the much lower price. 'This pair has the same last, so it should be the right fit.'

'Greer, come here, darling, I want you to try some other shoes on, maybe even prettier!'

Curiosity captured Greer. Ally picked her up, hugged her and placed her back on to the bench, then showed her the new boxes. Greer giggled on finding the raisin packet Ally had put in the recommended shoes. While she was engrossed in opening the packet, Ally removed the expensive shoes and put them away in the box. Picking up the second pair, she tried to slip them on Greer's foot, but her charge had arched her foot, obstinate on viewing the new offering. Ally stiffened. The battle was about to start.

'Perhaps I can help.'

Ally almost laughed aloud. She was willing for him to try! On cue, Geoffrey started grizzling, so Ally moved to him in time to catch his empty raisin packet. He jiggled around, annoyed with being forced to sit in the pushchair. A few raisins lay scattered like sheep droppings on the charcoal-grey plush pile carpet by the pushchair. She bent to gather them up and put them into the rubbish tin. An indignant yell from Geoffrey told her his opinion. With practised skill she looped her bag into place on the pushchair and gave Geoffrey his Mr Kiwi. He gripped the soft toy, and Ally moved the pushchair to bring him into line with the assistant. Looking at the scene, Ally grinned, impish humour getting the better of her. Greer had tucked her feet under her little bottom and had spread her skirt. Not even a thread of a white sock showed.

'These shoes are a lovely bright red colour.' The assistant was apparently studying not the child, but the shoes. He inspected each one, then moved a spotlight beside a fitting, arcing its light on to the platform in front of Greer. He turned the shoes slowly and in the light they looked irresistibly glossy. 'I'd like to try them on your feet. You have very dainty feet.' His smile was a toothpaste advertisement. 'And pretty lace on your socks!'

Ally had to admit that the man could charm when necessary. He had swung to give Greer total attention, and her feminine susceptibility, even at nearly three years of age, swayed and swamped her determination. She wriggled, then stuck out one foot, allowing the shoe to be put on, looked at it, then looked back at the salesman. He nodded solemnly, as if she was buying a million-dollar picture. Graciously, clearly bestowing the favour, Greer pushed out her other foot. Fitted, she stood up in the shoes and walked towards the mirror. She tried a pirouette, then, seeing Ally's smile, she ran to her, hugging her. 'New shoes!' she exclaimed.

'Thank you.' It was an acknowledgment of his skill. 'We'll take them.'

It was a shopping expedition she would prefer to forget, but the mission had been successful. While she strapped Greer into the twin pushchair, the man tapped out the docket. Ally signed for the shoes and headed with relief for the opening lift.

There was just time before lunch to detour to see her friend Anne, to return the latest notes and books. They had met as eight-year-olds when Ally had moved with her mother, brother and sister to the provincial city in the South Island of New Zealand. Their friendship had begun over a sketch, and Ally could still remember their mutual pleasure at discovering someone else who enjoyed drawing anything and everything. At school, someone had dubbed them 'The A's, Alice and Anne, Artists.' Now they were nineteen, Anne was studying design, and Alice had learnt a considerable amount second-hand, by reading her friend's class books. Because of their size and their high cost she delivered or fetched them when she had the twins and the car.

The lift pinged, started and stopped its way to the ground floor and, freed, Ally took the pushchair rapidly past the enticing twins'-reach counters and swept out through the main doors. A distinctive, tall figure in a dark grey suit blocked her path, and she looked at him disbelievingly. The man must have run down four flights, yet he wasn't even breathing rapidly.

'Excuse me, madam, would you mind returning to the shop with me?' His tone was quiet but authoritative.

'Yes, I do mind,' Ally snapped. 'Why? It's nearly lunchtime for the twins.'

'I don't believe you wish to discuss shoplifting on the footpath.'

Shoplifting? The accusation rocked her. Numbed, she allowed him to guide the pushchair to a private alcove just inside the shop. When he gestured her to a seat she shook her head and clutched on to the handle of the pushchair like a lifeline. Impatient with the stillness, both children began to tap their new shoes against the footrest. Not satisfied, Geoffrey began to kick, and Ally leaned forward to place her hand over his shoes. She didn't want them scuffed before his parents saw them!

'Your boy is wearing new shoes too. Covering them with your hand won't help. They're from Tasman's stock—I can see our coding on the sole.'

'I don't understand. . . .' Ally frowned, wondering at the implication.

'It would be a lot easier on yourself and the children if you admitted you didn't pay for those shoes!'

'You know I didn't pay cash. You put them on the account.' Under his censorious stare she tried not to wilt.

'I sold and charged you for one pair of shoes, madam.'

'But they're twins! We bought two pairs!' Her voice was a protest. 'The docket! It would have the details for both pairs.' She rummaged in the carryall for her purse, but it had worked its way to the base and she had to remove tissues, clothes and Greer's much-loved soft toy, Mrs Rabbit, before retrieving the account folded next to the plastic card. As she read it her emotions hit the floor. The docket listed one pair of red shoes.

'I think these are yours.' The man fingered two scruffy trainers by the laces and dropped them on to the desk, the soft thuds a double accusation. 'To shoplift is bad, but to involve young children is disgusting! You knew a gap in the stock would be noticed, and you must have told the boy to exchange the shoes with his sneakers.'

Anger pulsed through Ally. 'That's an appalling allegation.' She looked round for help, but the grey partitions were impersonal. 'I don't believe this is happening!'

The expression on her tormentor's face told her he was convinced of her guilt. Her brain fled back through the incidents of the morning until she remembered the change of staff. She straightened. 'I know how the misunderstanding occurred. You've made a mistake.'

'A mistake? Me?'

She heard the indignation in his voice. He could think she was a thief, but she wasn't allowed to think he had made an error! 'We were served by two people,' she explained. She could feel the heat reddening her skin. 'The first was a short, dark-haired woman about forty, very pleasant. She fitted Geoffrey and went off to get a second pair for Greer. Just when I thought she must have forgotten us, you took over. You didn't write the first pair on the docket.'

'A mistake could have been made.' The admission was grudging. 'If indeed that is the case, then I do apologise. I'll have to tap out another docket.'

His shoulders were rigid with displeasure, Ally noticed. She was probably standing much the same way, or she would be if she was not moving the pushchair back and forth, trying to quieten a grizzly, ready for lunch, overtired small boy. At least Greer was playing happily enough with Mrs Rabbit.

'Mrs Thwaites?'

The man, scathingly righteous, had compared her signature with the card. She had been expecting the query the first time, but he had not checked the signature. His mistake again. 'I'm not Mrs Thwaites, I'm Alice Barrett, the children's nanny. You'll find from your files that I have authority to use the card for children's wear. I did explain to the first assistant.'

'You will understand that your signature will have to be checked?' He was smooth, urbane and totally sure she was making it all up—Ally read it in his face.

'Please take a seat, Miss Barrett.'

She saw a mental picture of herself hoisting the burgundy bench on to her shoulders and staggering off with it and the double pushchair, and her lips twitched. Amazingly she saw the same lift in the man's mouth as he looked at the bench and at her small frame.

'An unfortunate choice of words,' he verbalised her thought. 'This will be attended to immediately.' He pushed a buzzer and a floorwalker appeared like a genie summoned.

'Yes, Mr Tasman?' The floorwalker smiled ingratiatingly at the man behind the table. 'A card check? Certainly, Mr Tasman.'

Tasman of Tasman's. The name fitted. He might be working as a shoe salesman, but he had 'Mr Establishment' written all over him. He'd probably gone to university, completed an accountancy degree and been given a world trip by his doting parents and was now doing a pressure-cooker course in retailing at the family firm. Ally could just imagine him telling his friends how he had caught a woman trying to get two free pairs of shoes; the first by using someone else's card, the second by switching new shoes with old sneakers!

The man busied himself with a file, and Ally wondered if he was checking to see if she had been suspected of shoplifting before. Anger and irritation threatened her. After several moments she decided that the floorwalker could have checked a dozen cards. An indignant wail from Greer as Geoffrey pinched Mrs Rabbit alerted her to the twins' fading patience, and she restored Mrs

Rabbit and handed Geoffrey Mr Kiwi. He grizzled and pushed the toy away. Mechanically she put it back in the bag.

'Ally, me hungry!'

'You may not be entirely wrong, Geoffrey, but saying so does nothing to render the condition any more pleasant for yourself or others.' She adapted the Goethe quotation, then saw the salesman was staring at her in surprise. Plainly he had revised his opinion of her literary capacity, if nothing else.

'Will this check take much longer?' she asked. Any chance to spend a few moments with her friend had gone; she would have to deliver the books and leave.

'If everything is in order, it usually takes about three minutes,' he told her.

The implication crushed her. What if her employer hadn't taken in the copy of her signature? She tried telling herself that Mrs Thwaites was a businesswoman; it was not the kind of mistake she would make. Minutes passed. Geoffrey grizzled frequently; he was a lad who liked his food on time. She had emergency biscuits, but hesitated, knowing the vegetables were prepared for his lunch. Another aeon passed. Ally looked at her watch and was dismayed to discover that the parking meter on the car was due to expire. A ticket would be the last straw!

She could not give the ticket to the children's parents; she would have to pay, and her week's budget was not designed for such a possibility! 'I believe we've waited quite long enough—the meter's due! I'll leave the shoes here. Put them aside and Mr or Mrs Thwaites will come and pick them up...if they still want to shop here.' Before the twins knew what was happening she whipped off the shoes and plonked them on the counter. Indignant wails from Greer rose to a full crescendo, but Ally, face as carmine as her ribbons, pushed the twins towards the door. The screaming reached siren level along the street, giving way to clamorous sobbing in the confines of the car. Ally, guilty for not explaining the situation better to the twins, tried to pacify the tear-racked Greer, but Geoffrey had begun wailing in hungry, tired sympathy. Deciding not to deliver the books, Ally concentrated on driving, relieved that the Thwaites lived close to town. Once home, the sight of lunch heartened Geoffrey; Greer pushed away her vegetables and continued to cry. Trying to quieten the child, Ally picked her up and cuddled her.

The morning had started out so well, the sunrise dramatic, layers of apricot and rose over a wash of misty indigo. She had delighted in the intensity of the colours as she waited for her mother to finish in the bathroom. The winter morning had not been too chill as she biked to the children's house, there had even been a tail-wind, so she had arrived slightly early to her usual rapturous, snuggly, if wet welcome from the twins. The routine of the day went smoothly, and she had been looking forward with the children to the trip to town. The Establishment Adonis, Mr Tasman, had turned the morning into a nightmare. He could keep his family's famous shop. She was one customer who wouldn't ever go there again!

The man had been expecting her to leave in a hurry. He had thought she was making up a tale about the meter! He believed she had pinched Mrs Thwaites's card . . . she could follow his reasoning as easily as if she was the one thinking.

And that was odd! Even with Anne, who had been her closest friend, she could seldom exchange thoughts, yet a man she'd met and disliked had instantly read her thoughts. The only consolation was that he would not have enjoyed the script!

Despite explanations, Greer continued to sob intermittently. Ally put the child back at her place, but again she pushed away her plate. After Geoffrey had polished off his own meal and his sister's, Ally toileted him, then put him into his cot. He was sleeping before she had left the room, so she went back to pick up the white-faced, exhausted Greer. 'Come on, little one.' She hugged the child and rocked her. Two fat tears trickled down Greer's pale skin.

'Darling, you'll get the red shoes—promise!' Ally decided her pride was not worth another heart-wretched sob. 'I'll ring your mummy or daddy and see if they can get them from the shop today. If not, I'll pick them up myself on my way home. Even if I do have to face Mr Tasman again!'

'Don't want shoes. Want Mrs Rabbit!' The tears spilled.

Ally was transfixed for several seconds, 'Want Mrs Rabbit' echoing in her mind. Rushing to the bag, she up-ended it, spilling the spare clothes, her purse and Mr Kiwi. Mrs Rabbit was not in the bag. The last time she had seen the toy had been at Tasman's office, she realised dully. Greer had not been protesting about her loss of the new shoes, she had been screaming at the abandonment of Mrs Rabbit!

'Greer—I didn't understand! I'm sorry, little love. I'll ring the shop as soon as I've put you down to sleep.' She could only hope the toy was still there. Minutes later, the child's sobs still breaking the quiet, she checked the telephone book and dialled the number.

'Mr Tasman, please.'

'Mr Tasman is not available. Can I put you through to his secretary, or will you ring back?'

Ally hesitated. Messages could get lost or overlooked. 'No, wait! Put me through to the ground floor information desk, please.' Piped music irritated her as the number was clicked over. Explaining the loss of Mrs Rabbit took only seconds, and she was relieved when the woman, understanding, promised to search the small interview-room. There was a long wait.

'I'm very sorry, but I can't see any toy. Maybe another child has picked it up. I'll take your number in case it is returned.'

Defeated, Ally gave her the number and replaced the receiver. In the other room she could hear Greer, whimpering. She went to the kitchen and set the coffee-pot on and made some sandwiches for her own lunch. She ate one but covered the rest, unable to bear Greer's pitiful sobbing. It was clear she wasn't going to settle. She went and lifted her, cuddling her close, singing a soft lullaby.

It was no good; the child was too distressed, her ribcage and shoulders jerking with each sob, her tears wetting the left shoulder of Ally's sweatshirt. In an effort to meet the problem head on, Ally began talking about the adventures Mrs Rabbit was having in the shoe shop. Every time she mentioned 'Mrs Rabbit,' the sobs checked, and as they lessened, she knew she was winning her audience. She pulled out her sketchbook and crayons. With quick movements she sketched in the background of the shop, the twins in the pushchair, Mr Kiwi and the counter. She could feel Greer's sniffing, as the little girl wanted to see what was happening to her toy. When the toddler wriggled into a seated position on her knee, Ally sketched more detail, keeping up a patter about Mrs Rabbit hiding in the boxes of shoes or peeping from the big potted palm by the lift.

With sticky fingers Greer brushed away the traces of tears from her face. 'Draw Mrs Rabbit, Ally.'

'You have to help me.'

Greer nodded. Ally drew in Mrs Rabbit, with Greer assisting her with the colours—the blue and white striped skirt, the pink jacket, the white body, one floppy ear and the embroidered eyes, nose and mouth. Greer even chuckled when Ally put in a pumpkin soup stain on the paw.

Greer was content, convinced Mrs Rabbit was safe. 'Draw man, Ally. He knows Mrs Rabbit.'

Ally roughed in the outline of a man's shape, but Greer was dissatisfied. Anxious to distract her charge, she obliged by drawing in the man's face, caricaturing the blue eyes, dark frowning eyebrows, exaggerating his nose, shading in yet unformed wrinkles.

Greer uttered a sound close to a giggle. 'You made man funny! Draw some more, Ally.'

Ally hesitated, wondering what she could do. She looked at the blank walls with the thin line of burgundy, then began sketching in a circus mural, exaggerating the animals and fitting them with shoes or boots. Just as she was reaching for another yellow crayon to finish off a nattily dressed lion, the small observer on her knee stretched out her arms, floppy as Mrs Rabbit. Alerted, Ally cradled the toddler and Greer nestled, her eyelids fighting to stay open.

'Ally find Mrs Rabbit,' she murmured.

Ally could only hope the infant's trust in her powers was not misplaced. If it had been Mr Kiwi, Geoffrey would have missed him but settled for another toy. Greer had difficulty relinquishing Mrs Rabbit for a wash, and Ally remembered the howl of protest when she had made the error of pegging Mrs Rabbit on the line to dry. If only it had been another toy! But Mrs Rabbit accompanied Greer everywhere, and Ally always checked that the toy was safely in the carryall. At least, she had until her abrupt departure from Tasman's! What if the toy didn't turn up? She could make another Mrs Rabbit, but there was no way to produce the loved rabbit effect without much hugging, squashing and washing.

The sound of a car in the drive deepened her distress. Mr Thwaites, a surveyor, had always stopped to see the twins for a few minutes when he was working in the neighbourhood. Lately his visits had been more frequent, and Ally was troubled by his manner. At first she had told herself she was imagining the change in his attitude to her, that she was being overly sensitive, that it was a coincidence that the last few visits had been timed for after lunch, when he knew the twins would be in bed. He had begun enquiring about her boyfriends and making suggestive remarks, then there had been the small 'accidental' touches.

Ally had been unsure how to handle the situation. She had mentioned her fears to Anne, who with typical practicality had insisted on accompanying her to a self-defence course. Both knew that before the situation got to that stage, Ally would have to make her abhorrence clear. Marital infidelity had split her own family, and she remembered the rows and arguments. She only had to close her eyes for the pictures to replay in her imagination.

After her father had left, the rows had stopped, the tension had gone, but the experience had seared. The intervening years had not softened her sense of being rejected and abandoned. As the eldest, she was aware of the difficulties her mother had and was still having, as a solo parent supporting three children. Ally knew the board money from her wages made a difference.

Although her friends had encouraged her to date, she had not wanted to form a physical relationship with any of the young men she had met. With none of them had she felt more than slightly tempted to forget her determination to find a man she could trust. Which made her reaction to the ruggedly handsome if obnoxious Mr Tasman all the more extraordinary!

The child in her lap stirred and Ally decided it was time to speak. Her protection would be the sleeping Greer; the man loved his twins. Mrs Thwaites deserved better; intelligent and charming, the children's mother worked from nine till four in her husband's office, administering the business. They were a well matched couple, and with the children beside them they looked a picture-book family.

Reality seldom matched fantasy! Like the Adonis at Tasman's! Fantasy would have him falling instantly in love with her, appearing to sweep her off her feet, carrying her off, not on his white charger, but in his up-market, late model car. The reality? He had thought she was a Raggedy Ann, out of place in his elegant shop. Instead of falling in love he had despised her as a thief. If she was lucky, she'd never see him again in her life!

She heard the man's footsteps on the porch hesitate and she glanced up, knowing she could be seen through the ranch sliders. Shocked, she knew her jaw dropped and her eyes widened in astonishment. Why was Mr Tasman standing outside? What could Mr Establishment want with her?

CHAPTER TWO

IT WAS the small toy Mr Tasman held up in his hand which sent Ally to the door, sliding it open. 'Mrs Rabbit! Come in!'

He appeared only slightly bemused by her greeting, glancing at the tear-stained child in her arms. 'You had problems?' he queried.

'Yes. You've brought the shoes too? Just give me a minute to put her down.' She nodded towards a chair and carried the child to her room. With practised ease she put Greer into the cot and tucked Mrs Rabbit into position. She checked that Geoffrey was fast asleep, then walked back into the day-room. Mr Tasman was standing by her open sketchbook. Embarrassed, Ally knew she had been cruel.

'That wasn't for your eyes!' she protested.

'You've a remarkable talent, madonna! I wasn't aware I was so fierce.'

'You thought I was a thief. Twice!'

'Yes!' His smile lit his blue eyes, making him full of charm. 'I've come to apologise. I went back to the shoe section and talked to the assistant. She told me that you'd explained that you were the nanny, that you'd been instructed to buy two pairs and that it was to be put on the account. I understand you pointed out a pair and she fitted the boy, then went to the rear to collect similar shoes for the girl. At that stage, I took over.'

'Why? I shouldn't have thought it good policy to interrupt someone in the middle of a sale.'

'You're right, but the circumstances were not routine.'
He paused. 'I believe you're entitled to know the reason.
The assistant's husband is in hospital and this morning
had to undergo surgery. I'd offered her the day off, but
she said she'd prefer to keep busy. The doctor rang to
tell her that the operation had been successful, and she
was so relieved she burst into tears. I knew the phone
call was expected, so I'd made sure I was working in the
vicinity. When I heard it was good news, I sent her off
for a cup of tea and I took over the counter. She'd
selected the black shoes, so I just picked them up and
looked round for the possible buyer. It had to be you.
Unfortunately, I knew nothing about the boy's shoes,
until I saw his sneakers looking like street kids' among
pristine preppys'. By that time you'd disappeared. I used
the staff lift to beat you down to the street. The rest you
know. The card was held up with a computer mal-
function. Before I could discover why the records had
to be accessed manually, I saw the toy. Greer's star solo
left me in no doubt about its importance.'

Ally nodded. 'Thank you for the explanation, and for
bringing Greer's toy back—she was very upset.'

'I have a young brother who was devoted to an old
teddy.' He looked embarrassed. 'I could have sent it by
our delivery service, but I wanted to see you. It's not
easy admitting that I blundered. I'm sorry.'

Ally decided to be forgiving. Mr Establishment had
to be human, if he could show concern for his staff and
understand how his young brother loved a favourite toy!
'You want my signature for Geoffrey's shoes?' She bent
and signed the prepared docket.

'Thank you. I'd like to give you this.' He reached into
his inner breast pocket and drew out a grey card with
burgundy lettering. 'It's a complimentary voucher for
lunch for two at Tasman's coffee bar. A token for you
to make up for the morning's unpleasantness.'

'That's not necessary. The apology is sufficient.' Her mouth twitched at the formality.

'Please take it. We don't want to lose customers. Both Mr and Mrs Thwaites have shopped at Tasman's for years. I imagined you refusing to bring the children in again.'

'You're not wrong,' Ally admitted. 'There are other places where they consider the needs of small children.'

'I agree. You'll notice improvements in the future.' He put the card inside her sketchbook. 'Peace?' His expression was boyishly pleading.

Ally softened to his smile, conscious she was smiling back.

'May I have another, closer look at the sketch?' he asked.

'It's not a good one—it's awkward trying to draw when you've a distraught child to pacify. But it worked.' She handed him the book, and as he studied the sketch she could see his expression change from amusement to appreciation.

'Really, you are clever! The animals are originals. I like the giraffe's red shoes.' His smile crinkled the fine lines around his blue eyes. 'The rotund little lion is smugly sensuous. Tell me, how much do you charge for your sketches? I'd very much like to buy this.'

Ally ripped it out and handed it to him with a laugh. 'You don't have to flatter me! You want to make sure no one sees such a caricature of you! Look, I could throw it in the rubbish now!'

'No! I'd like to keep it!' He began rolling it up. 'Why did you decide to become a nanny?'

The question surprised her because it came from him, but she had no intention of explaining her life story. 'Simple. I love children,' she told him.

'Those twins think you're wonderful! The kaleidoscope madonna with the golden hair.'

'My coat patches are like stained glass,' she mused, 'and my favourite toy was a kaleidoscope!' she chuckled, deciding to challenge him to admit the truth again. 'Right at the start, you didn't approve of me.'

'I thought you were about sixteen, ridiculously young to have twins, a child pretending to be a woman. I found myself wanting to castrate the guy who'd made you pregnant, and that shocked me. Even when I had time to study you and I realised you were possibly nineteen, I was angry. It was no use telling myself you were a married woman with two children... I could hardly concentrate on my work with the sexual tension between us. You have an aureole of innocence—all that golden hair... I wanted to touch you... But when I looked at you, I saw you despise me.'

Ally was startled by his admission. Her challenge had been picked up and handed back to her. 'You've been honest! I nicknamed you the Establishment Adonis,' she admitted. 'You're very good-looking and you've got a body a sculptor would want to copy. And you love it! The cost of your suit would keep our family for months. I don't know that I approve of someone having plenty while others struggle, but I'm not sure if it's my social conscience or just plain envy! I decided you'd have everything handed you on a golden platter.' A faint hissing noise alerted her to the fact that the coffee was beginning to bubble over. 'Excuse me, I'll have to switch off...' She fled to the kitchen and adjusted the percolator. The coffee smelt delicious. She hesitated. It was the man's lunch-hour! She leaned round the doorway. 'Like some coffee and sandwiches?' she asked.

'Please! Breakfast was at six and I missed my break. I had a difficult morning!'

She felt his smile spin her emotions into an unaccustomed warmth. It was the work of two minutes to add a couple more sandwiches and an extra mug. 'Not exactly the golden platter, but there is a silver spoon!' She put the tray down and poured out the coffee. 'I made a guess about your life so far. Private schools, university, Bachelor of Commerce, world trip. Now you're being guided up the ladder of management in the shop. Am I right?'

'Mostly. I'm the manager of our main shop here in town. Grandad controls the entire chain, of course. My parents and grandparents worked very hard, and I'm proud and grateful for what they achieved. But I'm not a free-loader. I worked part-time and holidays at Tasman's. My parents didn't believe in giving us every-thing on a golden platter, as you put it.' He munched on a sandwich. 'Just their time and lots of love. That's the real wealth.' He took another sandwich. 'These are great. Am I allowed to make a suggestion? Next time, more mustard for me!'

'I doubt there'll be a next time, Mr Tasman.'

'I'll make sure there is. And the name is James.'

'James.' She pronounced it with care, deciding it suited him.

'Try James Broderick! After my revered grandfather. He deserves it, he really is a renowned ruler!' James's laughter was a velvet baritone. 'Names interest me. Now Alice fits you—fantasy and olde-worlde images. Someone little with dauntless courage. The children call you Ally, and somehow that's right too. It's more gentle and playful.' He put down his empty mug. 'I'd like to see you again, Alice. If you have time between saving the whales and protesting against polluting the environment.'

Ally was attracted to him, but she was threatened by his powerful good looks and charm and alarmed by the strange way he could match her thoughts. 'Not a good idea. We're from different worlds.'

'You're an alien? Which planet?' he mimicked a small boy's wonder. 'I knew there was something unworldly about you!'

Her determination wavered, and to cover herself she asked a question. 'We seem to have a freaky awareness of each other's thoughts, but how did you know about the whales?'

He pointed to the sketchbook. 'You've done a couple of sketches in it for posters and banners.'

'That's private!'

'Sorry, Alice. While you were making the lunch it was too much of a temptation. You really are gifted. You should be putting your talent to use.'

'I like to eat, James, and I'm not good enough to earn a living from art.'

'You underestimate yourself, Alice. See this sketch? I presume they're your brother and sister. You can almost hear them arguing and laughing.'

She smiled. 'You're right. We'd just had a session on whether to save for football shoes for Jonathan or go to the movies.'

'Snap! My brother's Jonathan too. The girl looks like you.'

'Katie. She's the youngest, twelve.' Ally flicked to one of the other pages which she had spent hours working on. 'My family.'

'It's worth framing.' He looked at her. 'No dad?'

'Over the hills and far away. Good riddance.'

'He let you down? I'm sorry. Your mother looks quite a character, sitting here holding on to a rather ungainly teapot.'

'Mum's great. Respect, please, for the magic teapot; Mum keeps the money in it once the essentials have been paid. Hence the title! Mum is an astute manager.'

'And a gardener, by the look of the tropical rainforest in the background! Are those tomatoes?'

'Slight exaggeration! Mum was into organic gardening long before it became fashionable. In our case it was necessity. Dad hardly ever paid the amount he was supposed to send. Sometimes I get annoyed. Solo parents are criticised, but people seldom stop to think of the reasons why they go it alone.'

'Fair comment. You don't appear disadvantaged. I remember wondering which Italian designer made your coat. Did you buy it in Milan?'

'I haven't been out of the country. Travel is just a "one day" dream.' Ally picked up a crayon and corrected an unfinished edge to her sister's blue jeans. 'That's better. My mother is an excellent dressmaker and she taught us. I enjoy puddling around with fabric. Most of our clothes we rejigged from stuff from the charity shop. When I saw the three cotton dresses in red, olive and blue I couldn't believe my luck. Fifty cents each. The quilting I unpicked from an old dressing-gown. My patchwork coat cost me time and four dollars including the stiffening, thread and braid.'

'Not even the pattern from Tasman's?'

'No, I've hardly shopped there in my life.' It was her turn to smile, softening the barb. 'Too expensive! I work patterns out. I've just finished a course at polytech two nights a week learning drafting and design. It's fun! I like the jewel fabrics and flowing styles of the Pre-Raphaelites, but practicality rules. It's tracksuits and leggings and shorts most of the time. That's how I paid for nanny school training. I did machine outwork for a local tracksuit manufacturer.' Memory pulled at her lips. 'I swore I'd never make another tracksuit as long as I lived, and I didn't for a week! Football practice! Jonathan put his knee through his pants.'

'A lad that likes to live dangerously!' James's blue glance acknowledged her self-mocking laughter. 'My young brother is rugby mad as well.' He put out his forearm and the sleeve on his jacket edged back to reveal his gold watch. 'Time to go—duty calls. I can't be late back. I'll ring you, Alice.' He pulled at the narrow bands of red ribbons lacing her golden hair, freeing it to cascade over her shoulders. 'Beautiful! I've been longing to do that!'

Ally felt the power of his attraction, the laughing eyes, the easy confidence of his sexuality. He kissed the palm of his hand, then, tipping his fingers down, he blew gently as though to send the kiss to her cheek. His eyes, blue as the summer's sky, spoke a deeper tenderness.

Confused, Ally watched as he turned and walked towards the saloon in the driveway. Seconds later she heard the car start. She went to check the twins, but they were sleeping soundly. Returning to the lounge, she noticed that James had forgotten the sketch on the chair. She picked up the lunch crockery and began putting it on to the tray. The sound of a car in the driveway made her think James had returned for the sketch, and dumping the tray, she ran to the door. Her feelings crashlanded when she saw her employer, and she became more concerned when he looked at her and the tray, then walked into the main bedroom.

'Ally, who was that guy I saw driving out? Come here!'

Reluctant to enter, Ally stood in the doorway.

'A man delivering the children's shoes.'

'What do you think I am? A fool? Look at you! Your hair's all loose, there were two mugs on the tray and my bed's not quite straight. Don't try and tell me the twins have been jumping on it.' He was standing beside her. She could smell his breath.

'Mr Thwaites, you're drunk!' she said angrily.

'I had a couple! Well, if a delivery boy can, so can I.'

Ally felt him lunge at her, dragging her down, pinning her on the bed. Outrage conquered incredulity. 'Stop it! Stop it!' she shouted.

His whisky-fumed breath shut off her protest as he began kissing her, imprisoning her with his weight and sheer size, his hands groping, tugging at her clothes. 'I'm crazy about you. Come on, no one will know. Why not have a bit of fun?'

Ally wanted to scream, but she pressed her lips tightly together. Screaming would waste energy. Only the twins would hear her, and they would be unable to help. She began to recall the self-defence class. She should never have allowed him to use his strength to get her down, she should have broken his hold... but she was wasting time, and her attacker was fumbling at her bra. She had to stop him. Yanking a handful of his hair, she was surprised when he released her immediately. She spun to her feet and fled into the day-room. As she reached the door, she saw James Tasman lift his hand to ring the bell.

At the same time she heard the slam of the back door and the crunch of Mr Thwaites's footsteps on the drive. Shaking, Ally opened the door.

'James!' she gasped.

'I interrupted your little bedroom frolic?' His eyes were glacial as he stepped inside. 'Could I suggest that next time you pull the curtains? I came back for the sketch.' He stooped to pick it up and strode back to the door.

'No!' Ally said weakly. She heard the angry spurts of gravel and the roar of the car up the drive as her employer departed. 'James, it wasn't like...' Giant sobs blocked her throat.

'Come off it, Alice! If you want to play with your boss that's your affair. But don't expect me to condone or approve you earning a little extra on the side—or should that be on your back?'

He had slammed out, and Ally stared after him until she collapsed into a chair. She was still sitting there, trembling, when Geoffrey's waking noises finally reached her. Somehow she dragged herself through to the telephone. 'Mrs Thwaites, could you come home?' she said urgently. 'The twins are all right. I have to go.'

'Alice, what's wrong? You sound upset?'

Ally put down the receiver without even realising she had replaced it without answering. Shaking, she packed her bag, putting in her sketchbook and crayons, the box of her embroidery threads and beside it Anne's books. In the hall, she shrugged on her thick coat. She could hear Greer making up a story to Mrs Rabbit, and Geoffrey was singing. Outside there was the distinctive sound of Mrs Thwaites's car, the click and clunk of a door opening and shutting, then urgent footsteps.

'Alice? What's happened?'

Ally could not face her. 'I'm very sorry, but I must give you notice, immediately,' she muttered.

'Why? What's wrong? You're as white as the walls. Sit down, and I'll make you a cup of tea.'

'No! I must go—a family crisis. I'm sorry. Please give the twins my love.' Somehow Ally ran out to her bike and clambered on it, pushing the pedals hard to get up the long driveway. She didn't stop until she reached the park near her home. Wheeling the bicycle to a seat, she realised that in her haste to leave, she had forgotten her bag and books. Mechanically she flicked the bike's stand into position and sat down on the slatted wooden park bench. Hard-eyed, she noted the winter green of the grass, the goalposts for the rugby, the skeletal black and white beech trees, the pink tips of the willows beside the river, the blue of the sky. Blue like James's eyes. The tears began running down her face and her body heaved with sobs. Arms protecting her, she leaned against the narrow ribs of the bench.

It was some time before she sniffed herself to a state where she could pull her tangled thoughts apart, able to examine them. The terrifying moments with Mr Thwaites shocked her again, and the tears streaked her cheeks as she remembered the offensive kisses and his eager hands. She had been stunned, temporarily unable to move. But for how long? Ten seconds? Half a minute? Long enough for James, walking along the path, to see them on the bed.

With a frown, she realised that it was James's judgement which had flayed her open. How could he have made up his mind so quickly? Didn't he know her better? Anger with him surged and raged through her. She felt like marching into his elegant silver-grey shop and swearing at him. Kicking him! Hitting him! Hurting him!

'Ally? What are you doing sitting out here? I was walking over to get you to help me with a design, and I recognised your coat.'

Ally turned at the sound of Anne's voice, but when she tried to speak the tears overwhelmed her.

'Ally! That monster tried it on? I'll lynch Thwaites!'

Ally made an effort. 'He didn't rape me, if that's what you mean. He let me go when I pulled his hair. Or it may have been because he heard James arrive.'

'You've lost me! Who's James? What did Thwaites do? What did Mrs Thwaites say?' Anne stopped questioning. 'I'm being about as clumsy as a Clydesdale horse. Sorry, Ally. If you don't want to talk about it, I'll accept that. Are you sure you're all right? You look a mess!'

Ally blew her nose and managed a pallid, new-moon smile. 'You know you'll be agog with curiosity until I tell you! Besides, I'm over the worst. I bawled so much there should be salt water in the river now. Just don't mention James Tasman to me!'

'James Tasman? Tasman of Tasman's? Broderick Tasman's favourite grandson? How did you meet him?' demanded Anne.

'It's a long story.'

'So! Your first romance and it's over before I get to hear! You mean creature—you didn't tell me! I warned you that when you finally fell for some man you'd fall hard! Start talking—I've got until my next lecture at ten o'clock tomorrow.'

'No, you've misunderstood! I only met James this morning...'

It was growing chill before Ally had recounted the events of the day. She felt better for sharing her feelings with her friend, but realisation was setting in that she had given up her job and her income. As they made their way back across the park, Ally pulled a face. 'It was payday tomorrow—what lousy timing! Mrs Thwaites can claim it instead of my giving notice. I'm nearly broke and I haven't even got a reference!'

'You'll get another job as a nanny. No problem!'

'I'm not so certain I want to be a nanny any more— you get too close to the children. I couldn't bear never seeing Geoffrey and Greer again. I've been with them for a year. I started on their second birthday.'

'It's their birthday at the end of the week. Have you finished their duvets?'

'Nearly. They're so excited by their new beds. I've re-decorated their rooms—there were some brilliant ideas in one of your books. Oh, Anne—your books! I'm sorry. I'll get them back. I'll have to ring Mrs Thwaites.'

'No hurry. You should tell her the truth, Alice. But it's your decision.'

Anne opened the gate and together they walked down the concrete path, their footsteps and the repetitive squeak of the bike's front wheel loud in the winter quiet.

*   *   *

Ally drove her mother's old car down the Thwaites's driveway. Almost twenty-four hours had passed since she had fled, but her stomach became a storm-tossed sea whenever she thought of the incident. It had taken courage to answer Mrs Thwaites's phone call, although logic told her the twins and their mother were innocent parties. The news that Mr Thwaites was out of town had given Ally a gram of confidence. She wondered if Mr Thwaites had told his wife the truth. On the phone Mrs Thwaites had sounded subdued, but that could have been because the twins were asleep.

On the back seat lay the embroidered duvet covers, the best she'd ever made. Mrs Thwaites had purchased the fabric, and having the correct width had made a difference, the design being better without centre panels. As Ally pulled up at the familiar driveway, the twins came rushing to the gate ahead of their mother. By the time Ally had had several cuddles from the twins, the awkwardness had passed. With the children 'helping', the duvets were carried inside and they began putting the first inner into the cover. Mrs Thwaites picked up the second and began stuffing it into place. Once it was on the bed the room was perfect. Geoffrey dived into his 'Sea' with glee, his chuckles lightening the atmosphere.

'Clever, original and quite different from Greer's, with her gazelles and geese! Geoffrey loves the galleon on his wall. An interior decorator couldn't have done better,' smiled Mrs Thwaites.

'We can sleep in our big beds now, Ally, Ally—Alice,' Geoffrey announced. 'Mummy's going to stay home with us. But you'll come and see us.'

Greer was quiet, but she clutched tightly on to Ally's hand. Ally looked towards the children's mother, and seeing Mrs Thwaites' sad expression she told Greer to show Mrs Rabbit the new bed. As the child left, Ally spoke slowly.

'I'm sorry, I didn't want you hurt.' She followed Mrs Thwaites to the day-room.

'My husband and I had a lengthy...discussion last night, and he told me what happened. There's no excuse I can make. I'm no longer sure of anything. I thought the man I married was totally trustworthy... You are all right, Alice?'

Ally nodded. The woman in front of her was the real victim.

'My husband has some consultancy work which will keep him in Auckland for a couple of weeks. After that, we'll have to face up to the problem. I've rung a counsellor and booked us in—for my sake and the twins', I'm asking you not to go to the police. But if you did, you would be within your rights.'

'I think you've been hurt enough,' Ally said gently. 'And it sounds as if the situation is under control. What about a cup of tea?' Seeing Mrs Thwaites close to tears, she gave her a hug, then went to make the tea. The kettle had been boiled so it only took a minute to gather cups, saucers and milk for the twins.

'How will you manage?' Ally returned to the day-room with the tray. 'Kindergarten will take the twins part-time from next week. We've been along several times, and the twins loved it, Greer especially.'

'Yes. I'm glad of it. Short-term I'll work from home, as I was doing before. It's not as efficient, but... Long-term, I don't know. I'm having difficulty thinking at the moment. However, you'll have your own problems.' Mrs Thwaites handed over two envelopes. 'Before I forget...your carryall, a reference and your wages. There's a little extra—a discretionary bonus! I meant every word in the reference I wrote. You mean a great deal to the twins. If ever you'd like to see them, just ring me.'

On cue, Greer came running in, and two seconds later Geoffrey followed, anxious not to miss out. Their drinks provided a safe topic and, once finished, allowed Ally to leave. After hugging the twins goodbye and making sure she did not forget the carryall and Anne's books, she returned to her mother's car. Further along the street she drove to the side and stopped to open her reference. It was a thorough report summarising her excellent care and responsible attitude to her work, and she felt a warm glow after reading it. She tore open her wage envelope and saw the size of the cheque. Her brown eyes lit as she read it twice, to make sure of the amount. The paper enclosed summarised it; a month's bonus, three weeks' holiday pay, plus her fortnight's wages.

She was rich!

Elated, she started the car and went to the bank to deposit most of it, then filled the car with petrol. By the time she reached home she had sobered with the realisation that it could be a while before another job became available. She did not know what she would do, but she was no longer sure she wanted to be a nanny. At least, not to little ones who charmed their way into her heart. She had been lucky with the twins, Mrs Thwaites had left it open for her to see them, but a lesser woman could have blamed the wrong person.

'Alice?'

'Just me, Mum. Don't worry about tea, I'm taking the family out tonight!' She put the salary paper down in front of her mother.

'Mrs Thwaites realised the situation. Men! Just don't get married, Alice. Or if you do, make sure he's not a good-looking rogue who thinks he's irresistible to women.'

'Mum! I've more sense!'

'I hope so. Your father was good-looking and he could charm the birds from the trees. Love can hurt. I don't want you falling for some hot-air merchant without principles.'

'Not a chance, Mum.' She thought of James Tasman and agreed silently with her mother. James was so good-looking! And he knew how to charm! But he would never show the slightest interest in her even if they did meet again. He had judged and condemned her in a few seconds, and nothing she could do would convince him otherwise. So there was no point in thinking about him, was there?

CHAPTER THREE

WITH some hostility, Ally faced the elegant old building that housed Tasman's department store. From the security behind the wide windows, displays of spring fashions defied the wind and lashing rain. Pulling her bright patchwork coat more tightly into place, Ally admitted defeat. Tasman's appeared to be the one place in town where she could purchase wide sheeting in pale seagreen, the colour Anne wanted to match her bedroom décor. Ally had happily agreed to make her friend a duvet cover for her birthday, but she had not realised the promise would force her to shop at Tasman's. Despite the miserable weather, she had legged along, trying at other shops which carried bedding or fabrics, but routinely she had been directed to Tasman's!

At least, she consoled herself, she wouldn't have to go anywhere near the offices and a certain judgemental male! She straightened her shoulders and drew herself up to her full five feet three inches. Eyes ahead, she stepped out on to the road.

Red paint spun out of vision and bus brakes hissed as she was sent flying by a man's weight, the sideways rugby tackle crashing her backwards, although her body was clamp-twisted into a roll to cushion the fall. Pain tore at her as they hit the footpath. Crushed from the chest down, she felt her breath squashed out and she gasped emptily like a startled guppy. Opening her eyes, she saw, from shoe sole level, that the grey footpath held flecks of brown, blue, green, white and dots of red. The bright carmine matched her left palm where blood beaded along the lines of scratches. An inch away from her face a rainbow of oil formed a shimmering film on a puddle.

Weight rolled off. She spluttered dust, her breath normalised. Shock, anger, followed by the realisation that she had nearly walked into the path of a bus, mixed with flashes of pain from her side, knee and hand. Sounds penetrated, people clapping and cheering, noisy as a flight of squabbling seagulls.

'Worthy of an All Black! Great tackle!' The wheezy comment came from the wearer of brown cuffed trousers, about to board the now stationary red bus. Ally followed the progress of his polished brown shoes as he raised his feet from the footpath on to the silver and black metal bus steps. 'She all right?'

'She' managed to nod in the affirmative, and the shoes lifted to disappear from her line of sight. Sprawling possessively on the footpath, Ally was a reassembled robot which had to check if it could move. With her right hand she pushed herself up to a sitting position. The man who had crash-rolled her to safety was now standing over her, protecting her from the queue of bus passengers. She looked up to thank him. Blue eyes glared down at her. It would have to be James Tasman!

'What are you trying to do? Kill yourself! The sign says Bus Stop, and you stepped straight off the pavement without looking! How could you be so stupid?'

Apart from an oily stain on his wool gabardine coat he was unmarked. Ally stood up, ignoring his outstretched hand. Her knee and side ached abominably, but the scratch on her hand stung more. The left knee on her leggings had been torn, but her coat had protected her, the thick quilting absorbing much of the impact. Glancing down, she saw that two blue patches had ripped, and hung down like forlorn flags along the left side. 'It would be the blue patches!' she mourned, knowing she had used every piece.

'You could be worse off.' James surveyed her. 'Hospital, your doctor or our first-aid section at work? There's a nurse.'

Ally gathered her straying lipstick, pens, keys, papers, and put them into the bag. 'There's no need—I'm fine. Just a scratch.' She tried to be gracious. 'Thank you for your assistance—I think you saved my life.' Despite the discomfort of her bleeding hand she took out some money. 'You must allow me to pay for your coat to be dry-cleaned.'

'Don't be silly, Alice.' He shot the notes back into her bag. 'Next time, cross with the lights! Now come on, I'll take you to Nurse.'

Without giving her further time, he shepherded her to the corner. The buzzer for the pedestrian crossing sounded, and, as they were going in the direction she had intended, she submitted. Blood was forming a thin trail along her left hand, dripping from her index finger, and she decided that accepting a sticking plaster from his nurse would be easier than challenging his authority. In the meantime, she searched for and found a handkerchief, wadding it against the left palm.

Tasman's doors slid back with a faint hum and the warm blast of heat welcomed them. Ally noticed James scanning the counters, checking everything, and his pace quickened. It hurt to keep up.

'Don't worry, Tasman's hasn't been robbed by a team of nannies!'

The blue eyes read her antagonism and his mouth curved. 'May you be bruised as brightly as the colours of your coat!'

'Look, I can buy plaster from——'

'Forget it!' They were by the lifts and he waited for her to enter, then pushed an unmarked button which meant that the lift sped straight to the staff and offices level. They crossed a large storage area, and James gestured her to a seat beside a door marked 'Sick Bay.' He opened the door and Ally could hear the murmur of voices. Seconds later he returned. 'The nurses will look after you. When you're ready, ask her to point you towards my office and I'll take you home.'

'Thank you, but that won't be necessary.' She sat stiff and upright, annoyed that he was treating her as if she was an unintelligent child. From her angry eyes she saw James tighten his lips, but he turned and strode off towards a group of offices on the window wall. Left alone, Ally sagged, protecting her sore bottom and side. Before she had time to investigate her hand, the nurse called her and checked, anointed and bandaged. Released, Ally walked to the lifts. She didn't feel like shopping, but she knew that if she didn't purchase the sheeting, she would have to return. At the second floor, the displays of fabrics glowing with rich colours seduced her eyes, and although her muscles were stiffening, she moved among the fabrics, her right fingers pausing on the tactile pleasure of a sensuous silk or smooth rayon. A fan sweep of polyester cottons featuring romantic floral pastels in aqua, mid-blue and gold took her attention; the aqua was the tone and mood Anne had wanted. It was not sheeting width, but she knew she could cut panels to make mix-and-match pillows and edge the valance as well as trimming the sea-green duvet cover. Picturing Anne's delight, she moved along to find the aqua sheeting, hoping the shade would match. The colour exact, Ally checked the price. The cost was ten cents a metre less than the same plain quality elsewhere, and her perception of Tasman's as expensive jolted. As the assistant measured the cut, Ally studied the fabric prices and decided that either she had been wrong or Tasman's had become more competitive. The variety and colours of thread impressed, the type she preferred was available in the exact tone, so she added the reels, then wrote a cheque. Carting the large, heavy parcel one-handed would be the next problem.

'I'll carry that!' James Tasman intervened. 'Are you ready to go home now?'

'Yes,' Ally admitted. 'But I can catch the bus.'

'You've just turned the colour of the walls! You've had enough of buses for one day. Stop being so stubbornly independent. I want to talk to you.'

'To me?' She looked at him with surprise. 'There's more to it, isn't there? You don't even approve of me.'

'That's not the issue. I admire your talent. My car's out the back.'

'You have children?' The possibility surprised her.

'Give me a break! The shop's my baby at the moment.'

They had reached the car and he flicked the key to unlock it, before opening the door for her. The gleaming leather made an impression of supreme comfort, and with the numbness of shock wearing off her battered side, Ally appreciated the seat. She gave him her address, and only as they headed in the direction of her home did she notice he was wearing a different coat.

'Tasman's have an excellent reputation in menswear,' he had caught her observation. 'It's part of my job to keep it that way. Talking of jobs, my secretary has tried to contact you at the Thwaites' number, but there was no reply.'

'Probably at kindergarten. I don't work there any more.' She saw his expression, and his thoughts were clear; she deserved dismissal.

'You'll miss the twins.'

'Yes, but I'll visit them often.'

'Really?' His tone was sarcastic disbelief.

'You misinterpreted what you saw.' She was suddenly tired, with little energy left to counter his opinion. 'You wanted to talk to me.'

'It's part of my brief to improve sales and marketing.'

'I don't know anything about retailing.' Shock jerked her as a car turned without a signal in front of them, but James manoeuvred smoothly to avoid it. His reflexes were fast.

'You see it from the customer's point of view, and your interpretation came across in your sketch,' he explained. 'Instinctively, you decorated the plain walls with animals having fun trying on shoes. Why?'

She had forgotten the sketch she had drawn for Greer.

'Shopping should be fun! Especially with children. Anthropomorphism is objectionable with real animals, but if I can amuse a child with a cartoon then I will. Even a picture can distract or pacify a fretful child. Some shops seem designed to stress little ones and their parents.'

'Forget the shoplifting accusations, just tell me your thoughts on buying the twins' shoes. The truth?'

Her bright gold curls tossed and shivered. 'You won't like it.' Seeing his grimace, she shrugged her shoulders. 'The elegant silver-grey might do a lot for some, but it did nothing for the twins and me. The décor was intimidating rather than welcoming.' Ally decided she had been harsh enough.

'Stock?' he prompted.

'You had everything the twins would need,' she conceded, 'but in my opinion, it was basic and boring in its presentation. I can't see why it's not possible to have something imaginative.'

He slowed the car for the corner before her street. 'I agree. We're changing the store. Work has been under way for some time. In the pre-schoolers' area we have a problem. The architect suggested a mural, preferably bright and comic, but the recommended artist wasn't available. As soon as I saw your sketch, I knew your work was perfect for the area.'

'Mine? You want me to paint a few animals? You're joking!' She saw he was genuine. 'I suggest you hire a professional.'

'Our consultants tried. We also have our own art department, but no one produced work which was both original and suitable. Popular designs can lead to royalty difficulties. When I showed your sketch to Grandad he was enthusiastic. So, Tasman's wants to hire you for a short term.'

'A sketch done in a couple of minutes is a different operation from a mural.' As they cruised along the street she had time to absorb and dismiss the idea. The last thing she wanted was to see more of James Tasman. 'I don't think it would be possible.' As he slowed she realised he was waiting for instructions. 'The picket fence,' she directed.

He steered towards the driveway and stopped. 'Why not?'

'I'm looking for work.' She proffered the excuse. It was more polite than telling him she detested him for his arrogant assumption.

'I'm not offering you a paid holiday! The mural would give you a temporary income. We'll pay you double salary as a fee for the work and its copyright.'

'That's ridiculous!' she protested. 'I'm not trained! The only time I worked on a mural was at school! Airbrushes—noisy things! It's almost impossible to do detailed work. I haven't even that sort of equipment!'

'We can take care of that. Our art and advertising department could help with the donkey-work. You draw the sketch, Grandad would have to approve it, then you'd graph it on to the wall. A couple of our staff would assist with the spray work and you could concentrate on the hand detailing.'

'It's not as simple as that.'

'Look, give it a try. You should have faith in your own ability. I showed the sketch to various youngsters to test their reaction, and every single one began smiling immediately. Even my family laughed, though it was embarrassing having to admit why you'd drawn me with such venom!'

The quick sparkle of humour chuckled in the blue eyes. Ally found her reaction was to agree to his wish, but she remembered his use of charm with Greer over the shoes. He was a salesman, able to manipulate. Hadn't he tried and judged her? Now, because he needed her talent, he was prepared to overlook his own assessment of her character!

'We're not talking about the Sistine Chapel!' he encouraged. 'If you want to practise, you can utilise the back wall on the top floor. There's quite a large area behind the offices and sick bay kept for extra storage. There's not a great deal of time, though. Start tomorrow?'

Cornered, Ally shook her head and the blue ribbons jumped and jostled too. 'No, the truth is, I won't work for you. I know your opinion of me.' Her voice fired with the memory. 'You're wrong—I wasn't a willing participant with Mr Thwaites. He surprised and terrified me. I'm not certain whether it was his conscience, your arrival or my self-defence move which saved me. But you—you accused me of prostitution!'

'If I was wrong, then I apologise. But don't let personal antagonism stand in the way of business.'

If he was wrong? Ally snorted. 'I like to work with people I respect and who in turn respect me.'

'Like Thwaites? Listen, Alice, your relationships are nothing to do with me. You want a job. Tasman's is offering you short-term employment.' James let his seatbelt go with an irritated snap, eased out, walked round and opened the car door for her. 'Now that's clear, ring and arrange the details with the personnel section.'

'You didn't listen to a word I said!'

'Wounded pride talking is just hot air. I ignored it.'

Furious, Ally stepped out of the car, but pain stabbed, defeating anger with her aching body. Not willing to let James Tasman see, she gathered the parcel and the tatters of her dignity. 'Despite your opinion, I have to thank you for possibly saving my life, for the nurse's attention and for the ride. For that I'm grateful. Thank you.' Head high, tears prickling at the back of her eyes, the inside of her throat thickening, she turned away, her emotions as shaken as her ribbons in the blustery wind. She didn't want to feel any gratitude to James Tasman, she wanted to remain aggrieved, annoyed and angry with him. One thing was certain, he was a self-complaisant egotist!

'Wait! You can't carry that. You're as awkward as a one-winged pelican. Sheeting's heavy.'

'I'll take it, Mr Tasman.'

The cavalry arrived in the form of her brother returning home from school. Surrendering the parcel, she wondered how Jonathan knew the man beside her.

'You must be Jonathan Barrett.' James put out his hand. Her brother glowed at the recognition and with being treated as a man.

'Pleased to meet you, Mr Tasman! I've seen you play—for Canterbury, last year! You were great!'

'You play rugby, Jonathan?'

'Yes, sir! The wing's my position too. One day I'm going to be as fast as you!'

Ally watched with dismay. Her brother was not easily influenced, or given to hero-worship, but she had the impression that if James Tasman called for twenty sit-ups Jonathan would drop to do two hundred, regardless of the gravel and mud. Couldn't he see James was treating him with the easy *bonhomie* of an acknowledged superior male? She headed up the path. As she reached the house, she heard the sound of the departing car and then her brother ran up.

'Wow! James Tasman!' Jonathan dumped the parcel inside to hold up his arms in a gesture of elation. 'I talked to James Tasman! How did you meet him?' His gaze finally took in her appearance. 'What happened to you? Been in a fight?'

'Your marvellous James Tasman tackled me when I tried to walk into the path of a bus. Now I know where he developed his expertise. He probably saved my life.'

'Well, he would, wouldn't he? He's the fastest winger in the country.'

'If he's that good, why isn't he in the All Blacks?' She was bitter lemon, but Jonathan was dismissive of her sarcasm.

'Don't you know anything? Really—sometimes, Ally, you're hopeless! Probably everyone except you knows that his father died midway through last season. James had to give rugby up because he couldn't put the amount of time into it. When I was at coaching school in May, I asked the seniors' coach about it, and he reckoned James would have made the All Blacks. Said it was a "real sacrifice, because Tasman's was going down the gurgler".' Jonathan frowned. 'The shops are still there, so I guess James has made everything OK.'

'Someone should tell you not to repeat gossip.' Ally decided to change the subject. 'Thanks for bringing in my parcel. Would you put it in the sewing-room? What homework have you to do?'

Jonathan's disappearance guaranteed, she went to investigate the sounds of her mother's and Katie's laughter coming from the laundry. The smell of onion skins and gum leaves blasted her when she opened the door.

'I wanted a yellow-brown,' a giggling Katie informed her, holding up a wet, blackened garment.

'But somehow something went wrong!' Their mother's smiles dropped away. 'Ally—look at you! What happened?'

It was some time before she could shut herself into the outside sewing-room to plan the designs and layout for Anne's bedroom. Alone, she stared blankly at the fabric, her mind constantly focusing on James Tasman. She could see the trendy hairstyle, the smiling blue eyes, the clean, healthy skin, and her nostrils tingled at the memory of his subtle aftershave. Very expensive after-shave and matching cologne, she added, as she let the tape measure slip. Jonathan's comments had proved her right.

Hadn't she guessed playing fields rather than executive suites the first time she had seen him? His rugged, big build was the result not just of nature, but of hours devoted to intense training. To play for one of the top provincial sides he had to be good. If he had been considered for All Black level, then he had been very good, among the top twenty-six in the world. Yet, if Jonathan's quote was right, he had put Tasman's first, acknowledging responsibilities to family and staff, giving up his own dream. Ally frowned. She didn't want to approve of the man. She had been priggishly pleased when he had disregarded her ethics over the job issue. It proved her own moral superiority!

Her brow creased into a line as she recognised the flaw. Why was she even thinking of James Tasman? Sexual attraction? Was it just physical? The right combination of biological patterns? He was the type of man she had promised herself never to care about; a charming, good-looking puppetmaster. She sighed. Knowing the magnetism affected him too made little difference. From the beginning it had been there. James had acknowledged it first. Instead of giving the child's rabbit to a staff van-driver to drop off, he had delivered it himself. He had wanted to apologise, wanted to talk, to test the cobweb strands of recognition. He had called her the kaleido-scope madonna, the golden girl...his eyes held dreams... Mr Thwaites had smashed everything.

Wasn't it just as well their relationship had stopped before it started? She would have had few defences against falling in love with James, and such a romance would have been a disaster. Their backgrounds and their lifestyles were too different. Her pencil drew the small shadow above his right eye, the lustrous sheen of his hair, the straight nose, the sensuous curve to his lips, but when it came to the expression in his eyes she broke off. Even to sketch the man was impossible!

Undressing for her shower in the morning, Ally was startled by the bruises which had appeared on her body. She inspected their green, blue, yellow and purple color-ation, deciding that James Tasman's wish had been granted. It was little wonder she had been unable to lie on her left side without pain during the night. Persistent as the aches had been the thoughts about the man and the mural. One part of her suggested that as he had saved her life, she should be happy to paint a few designs for him. Against that was his accusation.

Dressed in comfortable old jeans and a sloppy jersey, she made some breakfast and tidied the kitchen. Her mother had a part-time florist's job, and Ally began the housework automatically. Aching as she bent, she took almost twice as long, but it gave her a glow of virtue when the task was completed and the advantage that she could sit down to sew without guilt. Her first attempt to control the fabric while cutting was painful, but she managed, and by mid-afternoon she had made the cover and valance and begun work on the pillowcases. Hand-finished, the set looked professional. Her mother, who had returned from work, echoed the thought as she helped to fold them.

'If you want a change from being a nanny for a month or two, you could make some of these and sell them. Why don't you talk to James Tasman about it?'

Ally's smile faltered, but she picked up the newspaper and studied the job options with more determination. There had to be something she could apply for in the employment section! Dismay crept with caterpillar steadiness as she viewed the meagre columns of Situations Vacant.

The twins' third birthday, the pair blowing their candles out with more luck than skill, came and went. During the first week there was plenty to do at home, sewing, experimenting with recipes and helping Katie with her dyeing experiments. The troubadour coat had been difficult to mend, but by cannibalising her carryall Ally was able to replace the torn patches and make a small clutch purse. Anne's birthday party had occupied another evening, and her friend's pleasure in the matching bedroom set was a fine reward. Ally talked and danced with many men at the party, but there was none of the attraction she felt with James.

At the beginning of the second week she reviewed her situation. There were few jobs offered and other people with better qualifications, as the employment agencies had briskly informed her. In idle moments, her thoughts swung like a pre-set hinge to the image of James Tasman. At times she was angry, at other times guilty. How could she be so unlucky as to owe so much to such a man? Would it hurt to give up her pride and do the mural?

Defeated by the necessity of having to find work, Ally walked to the phone. She would do the painting, but she would take only the equivalent of the nanny's salary, giving him the copyright. Only as she pressed the buttons did it occur to her that she might be too late! It was almost a relief when Tasman's personnel manager advised her to call, ready to work, the next morning at nine o'clock. She hadn't needed to speak to James!

The clock was pointing to nine when she made her way to the top floor and passed Accounts and Enquiries to the door marked 'Personnel.'

'You must be Alice Barrett. Welcome to Tasman's.' The older woman introduced herself, then handed over several papers. 'Read and sign these and fill in the top form, please. You'll be working on the back wall for a few days. The items you need to begin are there. Later on I'll introduce you to the head of Art and Advertising and the head of Hardware. They should be able to assist as you need other materials.'

Alice took the papers, filled in the basic details and read the contract of casual employment. Details of the copyright and the fee were stated, so she amended it, writing in the amount she had received for one week's work as a nanny. Pride repaired by the adjustment, she signed and handed the papers back to the woman, who showed her the staff washroom and toilets, then led her to the back storage area and the blank wall.

Stacked against the flat south wall was a painter's scaffolding, an air-compressor with a spray gun, colours and mask, a pile of graph paper, a box of thick pencils and crayons. The white wall invited her to spray graffiti cartoons of James Tasman on the plain surface. Resisting the temptation, she removed her coat, then began to prepare a grid. It took considerable time, and she wished she had asked James for the measurement of the mural.

Vaguely she was aware of people occasionally working in the storage area behind her, but it was not until a shadow fell like a caricature on the wall that she stopped.

'Thank you for coming, Alice.' James Tasman stood a few feet away. 'Do you need any more materials?'

'No, thank you,' Ally was as formal, 'not at this stage.' She couldn't see his expression against the sunlight behind him. 'But I do have a problem. Until I know the site and the measurements, I can't work out the design.'

'You'd better see the plans. In my office.'

She followed his lead across the storage area to the open door which gave on to the corridor of offices. At the end, he ushered her into a large room opening into an octagonal meeting area, and it took her a moment to realise that it was the turret corner of the Tasman's block. She had always liked the architectural jewel on the old building, and to find herself at its centre, looking down on the streets and market square, was fascinating. She was glad James was busying himself at a locked file; it gave her time to observe his habitat, the wide desk, the modern chairs covered in leather, the computer with its monitor showing columns of figures, a collection of advertising posters pinned on to a board.

James sat at the computer and placed in the disk he had taken from the file. 'I must ask you to keep anything you see in this office confidential, Alice.' He waited for her assent. 'We're redesigning Tasman's into a mall. There's going to be an entire floor to make a more practical area for babies up to pre-schoolers. Have a look over my shoulder.' He tapped the keys and the switchboard changed to coloured plans.

Ally studied the screen, listening as James pointed out features. 'It's impressive,' she agreed. 'I approve the safe play area!'

'Yes, you were spot-on with your assessment. Shopping is a number one leisure activity—it should be enjoyable.' He pointed the computer's arrow. 'The play area is sited along the rear where the access is from every section and in full view.' He eased the chair back as he flicked the keys once more and the screen blanked. 'That's the wall where you'll paint your mural.'

'The back wall?' Her brown eyes widened. 'But that's massive!'

'The same size as the wall you've got to practise on!'

'No! It's too big!'

'And I want sketches of the same characters linking the partitions between the various sections.'

'But I can't do that! I'd be a grey-haired old woman before it's finished!' Appalled, she remembered the papers she had signed. Could she have committed herself to the mural without checking the size? And she had written in one week's salary! 'I had no idea it was to be on such a scale.'

'Yes, I rather gathered that. Personnel told me you'd altered the terms of the contract. Pride and necessity clashing?'

'I have to earn a living,' she muttered, wishing his blue eyes were not so full of tender mirth. 'I decided to...'

'...Compromise by accepting a minimum and giving me the cost of the copyright for saving your life?'

Ally dragged her glance from the thick carpet back to his face. The sweet curve of his mouth set her thoughts at a dangerous tangent. She pulled herself upright, stepping back as James stood up.

'Oh, Ally! Don't you see that the fact that you have to work for your pay forces me to apologise? I'm sorry I hurt you. I've no excuse. That afternoon, when I saw you on the bed with a man...I almost lost control. I've never been so angry.' James paced towards the end of the desk before turning back. 'Primitive passion! With you, my common sense seems to be thrown out of gear. Just when I should have been sensitive and supportive, I acted like a jealous idiot.'

'Yes, you did!' Ally agreed, forgiving him instantly. He looked so ashamed she smiled. 'Please, don't crawl any further under the carpet—you're just about ant-size in humiliation already. Any more, and I won't be able to see you!'

He gave a shout of joy. 'Darling golden girl! I've never met anyone who makes me react the way you do! I think I might be a little in love with you. Right now, all I want to do is take you home, undress you and make glorious love with you.'

CHAPTER FOUR

COLOUR flamed in Ally's skin. She wasn't used to a man being so direct and so definite. James Tasman was a man who recognised what he wanted, but as the other half of the equation she had her rights. 'You shouldn't say that!' she told him. 'We hardly know each other. All I know about you is scarcely complimentary! You jump to conclusions too quickly.' She was flicking through her memory banks for excuses, his expression causing her heart to misbeat and race. 'You mustn't touch me! Sexual harassment of an employee!'

'Not guilty! At least, not until we both sign that contract again. This time I've given you the salary of an artist on staff for the six weeks of your contract plus thirty per cent for the copyright for three years. Believe me, it's a steal for Tasman's. Will you accept it?' He pulled the familiar papers from a manila folder and handed it to her. She checked the altered notation, then looked up at him. He was smiling at her, and his smile reached down to her toes, warming and delighting. She wondered what it would be like to be loved by him. Appalled by her thoughts, she clawed at the papers like a rope of rescue. 'It seems a lot.' Her voice was barely a sound, so she patted her chest, trying to cover up. 'Frog in my throat!'

'You're frightened of me!' James moved as though to reassure her. 'I know there's a Tasmanian devil, but I assure you he's no relative! Look,' he held up his hands, 'in working hours you're staff. Protected species. When you're ready to continue this conversation you come to me, clear?'

Ally nodded and bent to sign. She watched as James wrote his signature, the capital J and the large T overwhelming the other letters.

'You're now an officially employed member of our casual staff. Welcome to the firm, Miss Barrett.' James smiled. 'To work! Our paint expert has prepared the surface and is waiting for you to discuss the colour you want for the background wash. He'll need forty-eight hours to paint and let it dry. Once you've come up with the design, I'll arrange to show it to Grandad. The mural is to be completed in six weeks.'

'It's not long.'

'You should have started a week ago,' he reminded her. 'I'm confident in your ability. Go to the third floor—that's the new location. The manageress of the section will show you a model of the plan and the stock. It might help.'

She was being dismissed. For James a problem solved with a little charm. But for her...? To work on a mural on such a scale was frightening. She found a stairs entrance and ran down the flights to the third floor. Barricades had been set up to block off large areas and signs apologised for the inconvenience to customers.

Ally introduced herself and an assistant led her to the small office where the manageress of the section was working. Showing off the model of the new floor, the woman pointed out features with an excitement which she did nothing to hide, so Ally was not surprised to find she had been a staff member of Tasman's for eighteen years.

'James showed me your sketch! You didn't flatter him, but he likes a joke. And the animals—so witty! Made me think back! Years ago I asked if we could have some decorations to relieve the depressing grey but nothing happened. But when James took over, he asked the staff for ideas and passed them on to the consultants. The shop's going to be the best in New Zealand again. Now, I'll take you round the stock...'

Displays of cobweb-fine shawls, christening gowns, bibs, bootees, exquisite smocked dresses and suits took Ally's attention, but her ideas, normally plentiful, had fled. Time and again she visualised James's blue eyes as he told her he was almost in love with her. The thought was always closely followed by the declaration that he wanted to make love to her. Somehow the baby's cot she had sketched had changed into a kingsized bed. By the time they had reached the end of the babywear and toddler section the page was safely covered with pictures of dresses and shorts.

'It's lunchtime, we'll stop now. Come to the cafeteria,' the manageress invited. 'My treat, I'm so pleased to have you!'

'I'd like to, but I've packed a cut lunch!'

'Give it to the sparrows! Come on, I'll introduce you to some of the others. Don't worry, staff get a discount. It won't break my pay packet.'

Ally met many of the senior staff and enjoyed the company and the crisp salad she ordered. As she finished her last mouthful her lettuce became cardboard. James Tasman had entered the room with the most beautiful blonde-haired woman Ally had ever seen.

'Reminds me of a porcelain vase, that one. Fine line, expensive, cold and empty,' the children's manageress commented *sotto voce* as they made their way upstairs to the children's section. 'James deserves better. Have you met his family?' On Ally's negative shake she smiled. 'You will! I've a lot of time for old Broderick, he's the original trader! An eye for a bargain and business! A tough character, but straight as a kauri. His son died last year—lovely man, but, between ourselves, no talent for business. James took over a mess. But is he working! It's no wonder the figures are improving. He's determined to make Tasman's flourish, the stocks improved in range and price...'

A scream from a carpenter's saw cut off her speech as they reached the third floor. When the noise sobbed away the manageress closed her eyes theatrically. 'Another six weeks of the noise!' She allowed herself a loud sigh, then headed towards the toy section. 'I'll leave you here, Alice. Anything you want, just ask! I was told to look after you.'

'Thank you very much.' Ally's smile faltered and she pulled her sketchbook from her bag with jerky movements. Why should she be so upset because James Tasman had lunch with a beautiful woman? Hadn't she known as soon as she met him that his looks and charm were a trap? Why was she worried? What did she care? Perhaps he deserved his 'porcelain vase'!

A teddy bear stared glassily at her and she picked him up, comforted by the squishy, soft body. She had made one like it for Katie, years earlier, and it still sat on Katie's bed. Her own favourite had been a white rabbit with a purple and gold waistcoat and grey trousers, but it had disappeared when they had moved, and she had mourned it. She selected a pencil and began to sketch the teddy bear, and after a pause she sketched in her old rabbit.

As though her pencil had conjured him up, she saw a large white rabbit sitting on a chair. He was a magnificent toy, almost two feet tall, dressed in pinstriped grey and black trousers, a red and black waistcoat and grey morning coat. Unable to resist, Ally hugged him, then inspected him, appreciating his gold fob watch, which was actually working. The price tag in his top pocket was evidence that he was no ordinary toy. With reluctance, she settled him back on the chair. She was tempted to buy him, but morose sanity reminded her of other priorities. She looked around at the rest of the toys, realising there were some which never dated. Wasn't that what she needed? The mural would possibly be on view for several years, and fashion would change in that period. She perched herself on a chair at a miniature desk and began sketching some of the toys. Customers approached and she realised she was in the way. It took a moment to ask if she could borrow the white rabbit and several toys. As she placed them in a row to take upstairs, she wondered about a friezelike pattern just above head height, but remembered the size of the walls. She needed a forest, not a frieze, to fill the wall!

A forest and toys, perhaps a picnic? The idea grew. In the distance she could set mountains, the bush with giant trees, add a stream and, slightly off centre, a large, grassy picnic area. She hesitated before mentally adding small houses, trails through the bush along which ran teddy bears, rabbits and dogs, while parrots and rainbow lorikeets swung above. At the picnic spot she could copy the toy equipment Tasman's had available for the children, slides, merry-go-rounds, rocking-horses, rocket ships...

Arms full, she ran upstairs to her practice wall. Spreading her coat, she set up the toys on it; most would not soil easily, but James Tasman would not have cause to complain about marks on the white rabbit's fur! Satisfied she had protected them from any dust, she spread out sheets of graph paper and began to rough in outlines. After she had worked out several possibilities she selected one and began on the details. Several times she lay full stretch on the floor to redraw earlier sections, fitting her design to the wall key points. The adrenalin was soaring as she started mapping in the major sections, and although cautious the first time she climbed the scaffolding, she was soon scrambling up and down as she set the positions of the giant trees.

Darkness halted her in mid-stride as she was about to mount the scaffold again. She clutched the frame while her eyes took long seconds to adjust to the switching off of the lights. Heart-thumping beats later, she could make out dim outlines, the large, arched windows allowed a glow from the street lamps outside. She flexed her right wrist, aching from clutching a crayon for so long, then noticed the silence. Her fingers rubbing her hand sounded like a thousand whispers. How could a busy department store be so quiet? The hum of vacuum cleaners she had heard earlier had stopped. She glanced at her watch. Seven-fifteen.

Seven-fifteen! But the shop closed at five-thirty! She was probably alone in the building, except for the person, probably a cleaner, who had switched off the lights. She had seconds in which to attract their attention. 'Wait! Please!' her voice quavered. Telling herself not to be a wimp, she yelled, 'Lights!' Her voice reverberated. She realised that the person might have switched a master control by a door on the ground level five floors down. 'Help!' The sound was a scream hinting at her fright. 'Put the lights on!'

The shadows across the white rabbit seemed to have set a mischievous grin on his face which reminded her of James Tasman, and the thought stopped her incipient panic. 'Yes, he'll think it's funny too!' she murmured, looking at the white rabbit. 'But it's not so amusing to me! And it was the Cheshire Cat who had the grin too!' Rubbing her hands along her crossed arms, she noticed that the heating was also switched off, something that had possibly occurred earlier but which she was just beginning to feel. She would have to put on her coat. If she held on to the white rabbit to keep it clean it wouldn't matter about the other toys.

'You're coming with me, my friend,' she told the rabbit. 'All we do is cross to the lift, push the button for Ground, and there I'll be able to let myself out of the building. At least, I hope it's as simple as that.' She scrabbled her papers together and put her book and pencil into her carryall. Singing to convince herself of her bravery, she moved confidently until she reached the dark area shaded by the offices. Her voice quivered to a stop as she paused before edging into the thick black, her eyes adjusting, greedy for light. Gulping for breath, she reminded herself that she had crossed the area several times; it would be approximately twenty steps before she reached the lifts or if she had not kept straight, the swing doors shutting off the stairs. Clutching the rabbit, and using the other arm in front of her to sweep the air for unknown objects, she stepped forward with snail-like caution. After five steps she paused. Her wildly waving feeler had encountered nothing, but she sensed the presence of a large object. Her imagination cartooning ferociously, she shuffled forward, stifling a scream as her shoe touched something. Heart pounding a drum tattoo, fingers prodding the air with fearful stabs, she bent to her knees, until she hit a large prone object, unyielding yet soft. Her mind rioting with gothic possibilities, she forced her quivering fingers to feel the shape again. Wool, coarse, tufted, a heavy weave, then the same repeated. She gasped, then panted with relief, realising it was a roll of carpet. Hadn't she noticed several rolls in a line with the lifts earlier? All she had to do was follow them!

A few paces forward, a glimmer of light came from the swing doors slightly ahead to her right. Relieved, she charged ahead. A man's naked arm and outstretched hand floated apparently in mid-air, but her shriek of fright changed to a hysterical sob when it clattered on the floor and she realised it was the plastic hand of a mannequin. Hadn't she noticed the rows of display equipment and the shelves of 'spare parts' earlier? She stepped back, hurling imprecations at James Tasman. It was all his fault!

Determined to keep her imagination under control, Ally inched her way, until her right hand groped for and felt the smooth plaster of the wall. Following it, she patted the surface for a light switch, but failed to find one. The wall curved and her fingers jumped to the cold of the metal doors of the lift. She tapped along the side until she found the button. Jabbing it brought no familiar hum. The lift control had been switched off.

Despair eroded her confidence. The white rabbit looked back at her, his grin fixed as she played with the small gold chain on his waistcoat.

'Come on, we mustn't be late,' the rabbit told her in a squeaky voice.

'You talked!' Jaw dropped, eyes widening, Ally stared at the again silent toy. Reality and imagination collided for a fretful second until she wondered if the gold chain not only held the watch but worked a recording. Experimentally, she tugged the chain.

'Oh, my whiskers!'

She laughed aloud, guessing that Lewis Carroll would have appreciated her nightmareland. Cheered, she opened the swing doors to the stairs, and the flood of light from the stairwell windows encouraged her. There was more than enough light to use the stairs. Should she stop and use the telephone while near the offices? Ring home? Ring Tasman's? James's telephone number should be handy, but she wouldn't be able to read it unless she found some light. And near the offices there were bound to be security devices, alarms which would be triggered. The thought did not help; she could hear what James Tasman would say when the police informed him. Unless she rang the police herself?

There were other choices. She could stay where she was, curl up, go to sleep and wake up when the store

opened in the morning, but she was cold, and ready for
her evening meal. Triumphantly, she recalled her lunch,
and, knowing she had food, she felt her appetite subside.

The darkened area to the offices repelled, even though
she could hug the wall. The street-lit stairwell encouraged, and the hope that at the ground floor, she
could discover a way to let herself out. If not, she would
use the public phone by the information centre to
summon assistance.

It was half-past seven, only fifteen minutes since the
lights had been switched off, yet it seemed like hours.
Holding the rabbit and bag in her left hand, she gripped
the banister, stepping down flight after flight, pretending it was an aerobic class exercise. At the ground
level she sat, weak with relief, on the last step, eyes
blinking, dazzled by the lights from the window displays. She could see people on the street stopping to look
at the fashion displays, and smiled when she saw a couple
pause hand in hand. Thinking themselves unobserved,
they kissed, and Ally, statue-like, wondered if James
kissed his blonde girlfriend in such a tender way.
Disturbed, she moved. James had told her that he was
almost in love with her, and that he wanted to have sex
with her, yet an hour later he was lunching with a
fabulous creature who obviously was his partner! James
Tasman had the morals of a buck rabbit.

'Oh, my paws and tail!'

'Sorry, was I insulting you?' She poked the gold cord
back in its pocket so she could not trigger it accidentally.
'It's just as well I've been warned. James Tasman won't
even get within arm's distance.'

Keeping in the shadows, she began a systematic search
of the doors. From a few feet away she could see the
red light of an electronic alarm above each entrance, a
warning not to try the locks. Even the side staff door
had its own system.

Making her way back to the information desk, she decided to ring James and, if necessary, the police. She had to take the telephone book towards the main windows until she had sufficient light to locate the name and could write down two possible numbers. Back at the desk, she had a moment of fury when she realised the public phones were only operated by cards, not coins. The phone for the information officer set her scrambling over the counter. After a brief pause the number began dialling, and she prepared herself for the laughter she was bound to hear.

'Good evening, James Tasman speaking.' He had a rich voice, calm and relaxed.

'James, I'm——'

'A recorded message. Please leave your name, number and message after the beep.'

She could scarcely believe it. The sharp beep recalled her attention and she spoke with angry precision.

'James? Alice Barrett. I was drawing and the lights went out. I'm locked in the store. Please arrange for someone to let me out. Thank you.'

She replaced the receiver, wondering just how long it would be before James checked his messages; the prospect of having to wait another hour seemed suddenly too long. She checked her sketchbook, glad she had written down the second number, guessing it would connect to the large homestead Broderick Tasman had built out in the country. The number rang, then she heard the click of another answerphone. Reflecting that the entire household would scarcely be out late, she repeated the message.

She pushed in the numbers for her home, and almost cheered when she heard Jonathan's voice. Confidence regained, she did not want to alarm him or their mother, so she made little of the situation, but when her predicament was greeted with his incredulous gasp followed

by guffaws of laughter, she regretted her decision. She
would have liked some loving encouragement, instead
of brotherly hilarity. As for his accusations that once
she was working she was in another world, and his
suggestion to watch out for headless spooks... Ally
thumped the telephone down.

Glancing around, she saw the dimly lit outline of the
model house. It was one of Tasman's special displays
and featured the latest room settings. She could settle
down in the lounge and pretend she was in her own
hideway cottage. So long as the lights were wired! She
had experienced more than enough of dark shadows and
faceless mannequins and displays that moved when she
went past!

Leaving her temporary sanctuary, she set off towards
the display house. The outdoor furniture she could see,
but she almost missed the potted tub of artificial ger-
aniums until too late. As she walked into the open-sided
lounge, the light came on.

'Welcome to Tasman's world of interior decoration.
Our house is featuring the...'

Ally yelped, hairs prickling on the back of her neck,
then, as the voice continued to extol the virtues and skill
of Tasman's interior decorating, she located the loud-
speaker, not one of her brother's headless images.

'...look of summer, indoors and outdoors co-related
to provide a relaxing environment...'

Ally, far from relaxed, walked from the entry hall into
the lounge. More lights came on, and she stepped
forward and back, testing, discovering that her movements were switching them. She viewed the room, then
explored the rest of the house; the dining-room with its
informal setting, cane dining-table and chairs, the main
bedroom with its curtains matching the design of the
wallpaper, its double bed cover in a toning colour.
Positioned to be watched from the bed was a television

set, and she plugged it in and switched it on. The familiar nature programme was a panacea, and the tense muscles of her shoulders, neck and stomach began to loosen. If she used her imagination, she could be in a friend's home, rather than in the middle of a deserted department store.

Comforted, Ally went into the next bedroom, fitted out for a teenage boy. The thought of Jonathan in such a haven teased her as she picked up the books on windsurfing. In the kitchen, a poem of green and white, a recipe book showed mouthwatering pictures of a feast. The refrigerator had a range of enticing goodies on display, and reaching out greedily, she was already promising she would replace them when she realised that the chocolate eclairs and the fruit cake were wax. Disgusted, she returned them to the plate, then went to the lounge, but was deterred by the open wall to the terrace and out to the shop.

The sound of the television encouraged her back to the bedroom, and she viewed the bed with its luxury lacy pillows, duvet and sheets with indecision. If she had to wait, the bedroom with the television was the most comfortable place, but her clothes were grubby from the day's activities. She shivered and made up her mind. James could be five minutes, but he could be an hour. If he hadn't come at the end of the hour she would ring the police. Removing her coat, she laid it over the chair, kicked off her trainers and pulled off her sweatshirt and tights and dropped them on the chair too. In her kit she carried cleanser and tissues, so she removed the crayon and dirt from her hands before beginning on her face. As she did every night, she unbraided and brushed her hair, but she paused frequently to listen. When James, or whoever he would send, arrived, she wanted to hear the unlocking of the outer door, so she would have time to dress. She lifted back the duvet and climbed in, bouncing experimentally. Such a bed!

'Style!' she murmured to the white rabbit, as she hugged the duvet around her. On television a commercial oozed chocolate, reminding her of food. She reached the lunch from her bag and set it on a tray made from an interior design magazine, then placed both within arm's reach. Reflecting that the one fault was the lack of a bathroom and toilet, Ally restricted her fruit juice; the ladies' powder-room was on the first floor, and she had no desire to investigate it in the dark.

The nature programme finished and was replaced by a comedy movie Jonathan had told her to see. Settling back, appreciating the lightness and warmth of the feather duvet, she began watching, amused by the characters and plot, but in the commercial breaks her eyelids became heavy and twice she had to jerk upright to stop falling asleep. When the movie finished, she glanced at the time. She was just about asleep. All she wanted was to go to the toilet. And clean her teeth. She was so sleepy... so tired. She should go back out to the shop and ring the police, but it would be dark and cold... James should be arriving any minute. What if he had taken out the beautiful blonde? Someone in the household would have checked the answerphone. His mother? Grandfather? She pictured James's fury if his evening out was spoilt by a message to rescue the newest employee. It was a thought that brought a wide grin to her mouth, and she tugged on the white rabbit's chain.

'Come on, mustn't be late! Hurry up!'

'Exactly!' Ally answered him, and yawned hippopotamus-like. The benefits of a certain cleanser were being shouted out, and she wondered why the advertisements were louder than the programmes and with an effort reached out to turn off the set. She rolled back on her side and closed her eyes. She wouldn't sleep, just rest for a minute or two...

She was running along a path and beside her were the puppies she had drawn earlier. A parrot was screeching her name, and she laughed, knowing he was annoyed because she had given him blue feathers. 'I'll get some paint. Sulphur-yellow!' she promised. The monkey was calling her from a distant tree. 'Alice! Alice!' She sighed; she didn't know what colours to paint a monkey.

'Alice!'

It was the white rabbit, dressed in a dinner-suit. He was smiling just like James Tasman. His mouth touched hers, brief, gentle, a warm, clean masculine scent tinged with wine. Her name was a soft song on the summer's breeze. She reached out her arms to her old toy, cherished, loved, secure. The realisation that the white rabbit did not have a prickly beardline scratched her from sleep. A soft breath blew along her chin and left ear.

Startled, she flicked her eyelids back. Blue eyes were inches away from her.

'Oh, my paws and tail!'

'Mr Rabbit, I couldn't have put it better myself!' James Tasman was sitting on the side of the bed.

'What are you doing here? In my bedroom!' Ally struggled to sit up, pushing back the duvet, then rapidly grabbed it back.

'Kissing the Sleeping Beauty awake!' he smiled. 'I couldn't resist, you look so beautiful, your golden hair tumbling against your shoulders.'

'You've got your stories mixed up,' Ally snorted. 'There was no handsome prince in *Alice in Wonderland*!'

'What about *Goldilocks and the Three Bears*?' He put back the white rabbit beside her. 'Who's been sleeping in my bed?'

'It's not your bed!' She coloured under the deep blue intensity in his eyes. Memory returned. 'Well, technically. . . I was furious with you! Switching the lights off like that! You should have checked!'

'I was at a mayoral reception from four-thirty, so I didn't return to the office. Senior staff check their department, but you don't belong to any section, so I'm the one at fault. It didn't enter my head that you'd still be here working at seven-fifteen. There's an automatic safety cut-out which leaves only the display lights. I'm sorry. I suppose you freaked out!'

'Of course not!'

'No?' He looked at the toy. 'The white rabbit protected you!'

Ally looked at James sideways; laughter was simmering in his eyes. 'I was taking care of your stock. The rabbit would mark easily—the floor of the storage area is dusty. I'd put the toys I was sketching on my coat, but when the lights went out I needed my coat.' She was talking too fast, trying to ignore the rainbows dancing between them. 'He hasn't suffered any damage.'

'And you?'

'It's not pleasant having to find your way in a building without lights, especially when the dark patches hold rolls of carpet placed as traps.' She sounded priggish, but she had to hide the fact that her heartbeat was racing. 'It's worse when you walk into a floating arm and hand.'

'What?' His voice was deep, anxious.

'One of the spare mannequin parts—someone hadn't put it away properly. It dropped on the floor. I hope it's broken!'

He wrapped his arms around her, comforting. Nestled in his arms, Ally decided, compensated for any fright.

'Poor little Alice,' he murmured. 'No one had left a small golden key! At least you found your way down here to the house.'

'I didn't mean to go to sleep. You were so long!'

'Count yourself lucky I went back to the flat and checked my messages!'

'I rang the homestead too. Why didn't they rescue me!'

'School holidays. They're in Fiji. You should have rung our security firm or the police, but I'm glad you didn't. The sight of you in bed...'

She couldn't take much more of the sensual attraction. 'What time is it?' she asked.

'Now? Eleven-twenty. I was out for dinner. Yes, I do have a mobile phone, but there are occasions when I don't want to be interrupted!' He caressed a few of the curls on the sheet. 'Of course, if I'd known you were lying in bed, a Pre-Raphaelite princess, waiting for me...'

'Mr Tasman, you will please wait in the lounge, so I can dress.' She spoke with determination.

'Mr Tasman?' He heaved a comic sigh. 'There are times when being a boss is a distinct disadvantage! It's just as well, young woman, that you're only employed by Tasman's for six weeks.'

He slid off the bed and stood up, closing the door after him. Heart thump-dancing, Ally tugged on her tights and pulled on her top. Before putting on her coat she remade the bed and puffed up the pillows. She put the white rabbit in the centre of the bed, then opened the door. 'Should I change this cover and pillows, James? Perhaps I should buy them?'

'I'll fix it tomorrow. You'll be hungry. Want a meal?'

'I had a couple of sandwiches. If you have a torch I'd like to use the toilet.'

'I'll put the lights and the lift on. This way.' As they moved upwards he smiled. 'You must have been quite lost in your work not to notice the time.'

'It's a bad habit. Tomorrow I'll bring my alarm clock.'

'You have an idea for the mural?'

'I think so. Classic toys in a forested picnic spot. It shouldn't date too quickly.' She waited as he switched on the lights, then fled to the powder-room. On her return James was leaning against the lift. Ally breathed in deeply, striving for a fraction of the ease he seemed to possess. Back on the ground floor he led the way towards the side staff door and inserted a card switching an alarm control and the door-release mechanism.

Ally was shivering even before the blast of cold air. She recognised James's car parked on the loading zone in front of the door. 'It's been raining!' she exclaimed. 'The streets are wearing black satin!'

'And just as dangerous!' James chuckled.

In the car she took pleasure from surreptitiously watching James drive. She liked the look of his sturdy, groomed hands on the wheel, the muscular breadth of the man, the strength that was in his body. The dinner-suit he was wearing made his dark, vibrant looks even more appealing...but naked he would be magnificent to draw...

'Well?' James had stopped the car.

It took Ally a moment to realise she was home and that he had been aware of her scrutiny.

'You're very attractive. Too attractive!' she admitted, shaking her head. 'I should be interested in your character, not influenced by your looks!'

'My character?' His blue eyes teased. 'I'm honest, so I'll admit to a couple of faults. A black temper I can usually control, and a tendency to make up my mind too quickly. You've already seen both! In mitigation, allow me to say that I've been fighting a battle since I first saw you. My golden dream! Sometimes your eyes have the gentleness and shyness of a fawn, at other times the hauteur and independence of the tigress. Your hair is a miracle of long curls, sparkle and light... I want you, Alice,' he stroked her hair, his voice low. 'Tonight, I walked into my fantasy world...I saw you asleep. I

want to have you sleep beside me, to wake to the dawn
with me...'

The spell was winding her closer. She wanted to put
her arms around him, wanted his kiss, a deep, satisfying
touch.

A motorbike roared past, shattering the delicacy of
the moment. Ally's gaze followed its red rear light. Red!
Red for danger! James Tasman used words the way she
could use a needle.

'You've been reading too many of your own commercials!' She opened the car door and the light revealed his shock. 'Thank you for rescuing me, James.
Goodnight!' As she ran down the path she heard the
start of the motor, but he did not move the car until her
mother opened the door.

Wide awake, Ally was able to reassure her parent that
she had come to no harm; she could even laugh about
the carpet and the arm incident and falling asleep in
luxury; but she said little about James Tasman; the in-
timacy between them was private.

Yet it was the tantalising closeness of those few moments which replayed repetitively once she was alone.
She had deliberately rubbished his dream, and she knew
she had hurt him. What would have happened if she had
kissed him? Why was she shaking? Was it because she
was afraid of his attraction?

Logic told her that a woman would have accompanied
James earlier in the evening, probably the beautiful
woman he had met for lunch. He was ready to cheat on
her. Ally trembled. Hadn't he already proved himself
the same type of philanderer as her father? Her grandmother had a saying about an apple... What was it?
'The apple does not fall far from the tree...' Why had
it come to mind? Ally twisted her mouth, comprehending. Her grandfather had been a brown-eyed, curly-
haired charmer too.

Sexual attraction! A hazard which her grandmother, then her mother, had mistaken for love. It was the chemistry between James Tasman and herself, but it was not going to entrap her. When she fell in love it would be with a man who was trustworthy, kind, sincere, gentle, good-humoured...

So why was the white rabbit laughing?

CHAPTER FIVE

'ALLY!'

Legs swinging as she sat on the broad, thick planks,
Ally did not allow herself to look round, but tension was
revealed as her legs stilled, her torso stiffened and her
forefinger and thumb tightened their hold on the paint-
brush, although she continued stroking hair-fine brush
lines of sable-brown on the drawing. James could wait!

From her awakening she had looked forward to seeing
him and had hurried through breakfast to leave for work.
As she cycled along, she was champagne bubbling,
having to resist the crazy urge to sing as loudly as the
blackbirds. One of the staff had shown her the cycle
shed, and, as she walked to the staff doorway, she passed
James's parked car. Her breathing quickened, remembering. He had called her his golden dream...he had
wanted to kiss her, make love to her... And she had
wanted him too. The strong visual and physical appeal
linked them, the sense she mistrusted; yet the prospect
of seeing him...

During the morning she made excuses for his non-
arrival at her wall. He was busy, he was in a meeting,
he was serving—the list grew with the hours. By mid-
afternoon when he still hadn't bothered to visit her perch,
she convinced herself she had been right to deny any
attraction. Her mood had rollercoasted down, im-
pinging on her work, the certainty in the idea for the
mural had faded and she had spoilt the earlier, clear
outline by constant re-drawing. At three o'clock she decided that if she kept worrying the graph there would

be more pencil than pattern, so she decided to attempt a painting. Regardless of the eventual design, she had to find out how difficult the manipulation of the spray-painting equipment would be.

Warily she set the paint in place, adjusted the spray nozzle, pulled on the headset and, switching on the compressor, began work on tree-trunk seats and tables. The spray was alarmingly fast, but gradually she found her control improving, as she remembered techniques, and even began layering for texture. Seeking a more difficult subject, she changed colour before beginning one of the central figures, a handsome white rabbit. After some time she stopped the noisy, vibrating sprayer, yanked off the headset and viewed her effort with disfavour. The result was recognisable, but she despaired of her lack of ability. The rabbit's fur, instead of having a glossy, soft appearance, was flat and unreal. While she waited for the colour to dry she cleaned the equipment, pondering the problem of mixing the spray and hand finishing. Eyeing the rabbit, she decided to try hand-painting in shades of cream, sable, gold and grey to make up the density and lush beauty of the fur. Beginning on the paw, she stroked on some gold, and was immediately dissatisfied. Thinning one of the brushes to a few fine hairs, she began again, and after some time smiled at the effect. It was an achingly slow process. Her wrists and fingers were a tingling tenseness and all she had retouched were two paws and a floppy ear.

'Alice!'

The formal name; a demand for instant attention. He could wait! Hadn't she been waiting all day! She glared down at James. So good-looking, so arresting with his vivid blue eyes and smile. So sure of himself! Petulance laced with irritation at his interruption.

'It's six-thirty,' he told her.

'Is it?' Surprised, Ally glanced at the time. She had been right to douse the surge of happiness on hearing him call her name. He was just checking to see if she had left. 'Don't worry, I've no intention of being locked in again! I brought my alarm clock with me and set it for seven o'clock!'

'I'm leaving now, and so are you.'

'Feeling bossy? I have to clean my brushes first. It won't take long.' She looked at him, observing changes. His eyelids were heavier than usual, his shoulder muscles slack. 'Had a hard day?' she threw the question as she clambered down and tugged off her protective headscarf.

'I've known better!'

She cleaned her brushes, watching as James examined the tree-trunk seats and the rabbit. Her mouth twisted as she saw his frown. What had he expected? A work of art? The brushes in order, she gathered her sketchbook and pencils into her carryall, then went to pick up her yellow cycling jacket.

James was holding it out for her. He slipped it on to her arms and lifted her hair from her shoulders to free the collar. She was shocked by the intensity of desire that clawed at her, as his fingers brushed up the back of her neck behind her ear, the sensual warmth of his body close to hers. Instinctively she pulled away, clutching her jacket, then regretted her move. He had simply been helping her, a courtesy.

Rebuffed, James was striding ahead of her towards the lift, and she wanted to run after him, to stop him, to make him listen. 'James, I'm attracted to you, but you represent every man I've been warned against. When you touched me... how can I explain? It was like being in a theatre, the thick velvet curtains being swung back— but I don't know the words or the actions. I'm frightened...' The words remained unsaid. Stomach cramping, she walked across the floor. James was at the lift, he thumped the button and doors yawned. In the lift they were silent; James on one side, distant. Ally gazed at the flashes of numbers in the old-fashioned panel. The doors slid back at the ground level.

'I'll drop you at your home, Ally, but we have a small detour, to Grandad's place,' said James.

'There's no need, I have my bike.' She tugged her cycling helmet out of her carryall.

'It's dark and freezing. Your bike's in the staff space? Yes? Then it will be padlocked in by now, and I don't carry those keys with me. Besides, Grandad wants to meet you. I was meant to ask you earlier, I should have sent my secretary, but I thought I'd see you myself. Some unexpected business held me up. Do you mind?'

Before she could protest he had opened the side staff door. The cold wind sliced at her exposed face and un-gloved hands. It wasn't the place to argue. Her eyes were watering by the time she reached the car and sank into its protection.

'You were going to bike in this temperature!' James fingered away a tear dribbling along her cheekbone. 'The wind came up this afternoon, straight from Antarctica. You'd be an icicle on a bicycle before you reached the corner.'

His smile curved his lips and reached into his eyes, gentle, tender, as though he was trying to understand. She had to relax her hands; clenched fingers, white knuckles holding in her emotions as she was holding in the swollen contents of her bag. She shivered and he flicked a switch. Hot air blasted out from vents, and he grinned, a boy appreciating his finely engineered toy.

'Why does your grandfather want to meet me?' she asked.

'He wants to ask you about the mural. Just a few minutes, I promise.'

Ally looked lugubriously at her outfit.

'With that jacket you look like a dandelion, one under attack from rust and mildew!' He tapped the streaks of paint on her right thigh. 'Don't worry, Grandad knows you've been painting.'

A command to attend the emperor. If only James had warned her! She could have braided her hair and put on fresh make-up. Despite fatigue, James looked well presented, his dark suit and shirt impeccable, a pleasure for her visual sense. Why did she have to react like a fish to a dazzling lure? He would be just as treacherous.

'Warm again?' At her nod he flicked the switch and the heater quietened to a soft purr.

The cocooning luxury made her even more conscious of his attraction. She had to cover it with sound or James would pick up on her tension, as he had minutes earlier. 'In the shop I forget the weather,' she explained. 'This morning, cycling was great—ten degrees Centigrade at half-past eight, a fairy-tale spring day. Pink blossoms against a rainwashed blue sky. Fat brown buds on the trees along by the park, ice-cream mountains in the distance.' She was babbling, a stream of sound. 'Jonathan calls it my floorpolish song.'

'Waxing lyrical!' James's grin of appreciation deepened humour lines in his profile. He turned the car into a driveway and pulled up in front of a modern townhouse. 'This is Grandad's place.' He was already opening the car door. 'Come on!'

The freezing night encouraged Ally to hurry, and while James used his key, she pulled down her cycling jacket to cover the paint. The old olive tights were streaked where she had occasionally wiped excess white, sepia, cream, sable, ochre and red off her brushes. Inside, James removed his long coat, but when he looked at her she shook her head. Her yellow jacket was clean and a full-length mirror told her it hid the paint.

James ushered her into a pleasantly proportioned living-room. A fire gave a glow of warmth, but the elderly man who stood by the fireplace dominated the room. Tall as James, brigadier-straight, with a monastic hairline, his intelligent blue eyes smiled a welcome as he held out his hand.

'It's a joy to meet you, Alice. I told my grandson to bring you—I want to hear how the plans are for the mural. I'm pleased you were able to spare me a few minutes. Would you like a drink?'

'No, thank you.' She smiled, to soften the negative. It wasn't Broderick Tasman's fault that his grandson had manoeuvred her into the visit.

'Alice, do sit down.' Mr Tasman gestured to a chair. 'James, the figures are on my desk. If you want the earlier ones too, you'll have to do a print-out.'

'Fine, Grandad. Excuse me, Ally.'

'About the mural, Alice, have you worked out an outline yet?' asked Mr Tasman.

'I graphed one idea and transferred it. Yesterday I thought it was good, today...' She pulled a face. 'Bush, trails and an open space with play equipment. Soft toy animal families, classic ones like teddy bears, dressed up for a communal picnic.'

'Sounds perfect. But you've gone off the idea? Why?'

'I've been having problems with the trees. Each time I seem to make the bush too dark.'

'Is that your sketchbook? Can you show me what you mean? Use the table, Alice.'

She moved to it and spread out her book to a double blank page. Selecting a pencil, she began roughing in the design. James's grandfather stood back by the fire asking her occasional questions, but as the sketch was shaped he moved to watch.

'You can do more than draw water from a well!' he commended. 'There's a patch of bush near our beach house—a couple of giant totaras at the back, but the rest is rangiora, five-finger and scrubby manuka graduating to open ground. Go and take a look one afternoon. It could give you a hint on the background. It's eight kilometres down Beach Road. Come and see me before you go and I'll give you the key to the house, or get James to take you there. He could do with some time off! Talking time, I've taken up more than my ten minutes. James is in my study; the first door on the left across the hall.'

Ally left him examining her sketches. In the study James was standing by a computer, the printer whirring through figures.

'Won't be long, Ally,' he said.

It was a large room, but her attention was grabbed by two paintings on the wall, and she walked towards them. Light and shade, colour set to music, they drew her like an energy force. Unaware that the printer had stopped and James's grandfather had followed her, she continued to admire the bold paintings.

'You like them?' Mr Tasman asked the question.

'Brilliant colours!' She spoke with awe. 'So intense! They're like nothing I've ever seen!' A vague memory teased her. 'Usually you can tell the influences of artists, but the only one I can think of is O'Keeffe.'

'A discerning observation. When my wife and I were in the United States many years ago, we saw an exhibition which featured several of O'Keeffe's paintings. Alice was ecstatic about them, but I refused to buy one—too many difficulties transporting it from New York to New Zealand, organising export funds and so on. We had quite a row about it!' The fine skin around the blue eyes crinkled with reminiscence. 'It took me some time to work out that I said no because I resented the hours my wife spent in her studio.'

'These are her work? And you were jealous of her painting?' asked Ally.

'Yes. I wouldn't have minded a watercolour of flowers or portraits of the children, but she had no intention of filling a plastic mould! She was incredible!'

'You miss her?'

'Would the day miss the sun?' He looked again at the painting and back at her. 'When James told me he'd met a young woman whose name was Alice, and then pro-ceeded to show me a caricature you'd done, I almost heard his grandmother chuckle.' He looked across to his grandson. The old man's smile rested on James like the warm tweed coat he was shrugging into.

'Grandad, I'll do an analysis of these figures and ring you. Ally, I'll take you home.' James picked up his briefcase. He pushed some of the dark curly hair back from his forehead. The gesture was so weary that Ally ached for him. In the hall she quickly said goodbye to Mr Tasman, hoping he was not too disturbed by her name and the evocative smell of paint. As James drove she was thoughtful.

'You liked my grandmother's paintings?' queried James.

'Like isn't the word. They're impressive, challenging, full of beauty. I'm surprised I haven't heard about her.'

'She never exhibited her work. Grandma didn't have much time for painting—the family and the business kept her too busy. When Grandad decided to expand to a second shop she ran the first, and so it went on. Somehow she kept on painting, but she destroyed or overpainted most of her canvases. Just when she could have concentrated on painting, she became sick and died. Those two paintings were the pick of her work. Grandad rarely speaks about her, yet with you he was quite open.'

'Maybe because I have the same name.' Ally flicked away the observation, discerning that James was disturbed by it. He turned the car at the traffic-lights and they reached her home within minutes. As she picked up her carryall, she realised she had left her sketchbook on Mr Tasman's table. Her immediate thought was to ask James to return so she could retrieve it, but he looked so worn that she hesitated.

'I won't be at the shop for the next couple of days, Ally, so I'd like you to leave with the rest of the staff at five-thirty. Set that clock of yours!'

'Fine. You don't have to worry about me.'

He smiled, a basset-hound, pulled-down smile. 'Of course not! Goodnight, Alice.'

She opened the car door and sped down the path, running from her own chaotic desires as much as the cold. Inside, the greetings of her family distracted her, and later, helping Katie with her homework should have kept her mind away from James. Yet thoughts of him kept tugging at her, like the wind might flap clothes on a line, catching her, twisting her off balance, filling her and stretching her imagination wide.

In the morning, Ally travelled by bus to Tasman's, and knowing James was not going to appear, she settled to work, painting the rabbit. Its fur hadn't grown easier overnight, and it was almost lunchtime when she began on the clothes. Her fingers stiffened pegs when she stopped for lunch an hour later, she fumbled for her carryall and went downstairs, needing a walk and fresh air.

Outside, the sun was warm, the grass in the square a vivid emerald, and because most of the lunching workers had left there were empty bench seats. It was too early for the formal plantings to be in flower, but between the roots of a tree snowdrops had hung their delicate white bells. Entranced, Ally decided to paint them in her mural, but on reaching for her sketchbook she remembered it was on Mr Tasman's table. She would have to ring and ask if she could pick it up on her way home. Her sketchbook was like a diary, personal and private; she didn't want James seeing it—the sketches of him were too revealing. Her gaze was held by a Pop Art ladybird, black with scarlet spots, swaying on a seedhead. Minutely inspecting it from various angles, she looked round for paper, then unscrewed the paper bag which had held her lunch. Before she completed her first sketch the ladybird flew on to her paper, walked all over her drawing, then took off, leaving Ally chuckling at its apparent disgust.

She was smiling as she walked round the block and re-entered Tasman's. At the information desk the attendant made an appointment for her to collect the book. Returning to her wall, Ally reset the alarm clock, then decided to spray-paint a teddy bear. The fibre had to be easier than the rabbit's fur!

With each one an improvement, she sprayed three bears. By four, she had hand-finished the smallest bear, its grin cheeky, its black button eyes mischievous. Conscious of her appointment, Ally cleaned her brushes and her hands, then rebraided her hair, knotting yellow ribbons through it, refreshed her make-up and changed her old painting suit for pale green trousers and top. Remembering James's 'dandelion', she tugged on her yellow jacket and cycling helmet. Yellow was the most visible colour, and she wanted to be seen, not squashed by the impatient drivers. The square clock showed four-thirty as she cycled past, then rode along the river bank until she reached Broderick Tasman's house. She set her bike against a tree by the steps and rang the bell.

'Good afternoon, Alice. Come in! Your sketchbook is on the table.'

'Sorry to trouble you.' Ally followed him into the house. 'I've missed it!' In the lounge she took the book and, resisting the temptation to hug it to her, put it in her carryall.

'My wife used to carry one around everywhere too.' Broderick Tasman was smiling. 'Have you time for a cup of tea?'

Ally noticed the silver tea service beside a filled cup. 'Yes, please—I'm feeling as parched as the Hakataramea valley after months of drought! I finished my drink at lunchtime.'

'Were you pleased with the work today?' he asked.

'Yes and no! I'm experimenting with the paint and the figures.' As she described the problems, it was obvious from Broderick Tasman's comments that he understood. When he offered to show her some more of his wife's work, Ally accepted eagerly. She followed him into a studio which was set up as if the artist was about to start work, with a stretched canvas on the easel. Curtains shrouded the dying daylight, and when the lights were turned on, Ally was dazzled by the strong, colouful paintings which lined one wall. Absorbed, she moved from one to another, then back again. A movement alerted her to the old man and she remembered her manners. 'Thank you for allowing me to see them. With such soaring songs I have to be silent.' She smiled, lightening the moment.

Broderick Tasman led the way back to the hall, and Ally put on her jacket.

'Just like a daffodil!' The old man handed her the yellow helmet.

'A dandelion, according to James,' Ally laughed.

'He always liked dandelions! When he was three he picked a handful for his grandmother, and she did a sketch of the posy. One of the few I approved! I sneaked it out, had it framed and kept it in my office. Alice never said a word, but for my fiftieth birthday she painted me some dandelions.' Broderick Tasman chuckled. 'It's my favourite! It's in my wing at the homestead. When James takes you there, ask him to show you.'

Doubting whether she would ever see the notable homestead which Broderick and Alice Tasman had built thirty years earlier, Ally said goodbye and ran down to her bicycle. Out in the street, the darkness of the night was appearing, and as she pulled up in front of her own home she checked the time. Shocked, she realised she had spent almost an hour with James's grandfather, yet it had seemed more like twenty minutes. She had promised to be home early, it was her turn to cook, and Anne was joining them for dinner.

A day later, Ally had painted Mrs Rabbit and Mr Kiwi with the twins and spray-painted part of the forest when the alarm went off at five-thirty. She washed the spray gear and, returning, had a fresh, long view of her work. The bush was still not pleasing her, but the work was beginning to look like a mural and not an artistic disaster! The central white rabbit, in his immaculate attire, was passable, but Ally was not satisfied with the expression on his face. She reset the clock to seven and picked up one of her fine brushes. The princely rabbit reminded her of James and, unable to resist, she corrected body and head lines, extended the nose, widened the eyes and altered the mouth and chin. She stepped back with a laugh. Her caricature of James about to check his elegant hunter's watch was good! In the morning she would have to paint it over, but first she wanted to see it dry.

The alarm clock startled her; she had fifteen minutes to clean her brushes and get out of the building. James's secretary had given her a security release card and number earlier, but she had reminded her to leave when the shop closed. Ally grabbed her brushes and sped to the washroom. Why hadn't she resisted the temptation to carry on instead of resetting the alarm at five-thirty?

At twelve minutes past seven she let herself out of the staff door. Walking to the cycle shed, she viewed the gate with chagrin, remembering James had told her it was padlocked earlier. Muttering about security, she checked her bus timetable; one was due in fifteen minutes. In that time, she could walk halfway home.

A car pulled into Tasman's car park and power-bright headlights caught her in the beam. Vulnerable, she was conscious that she was alone in a dimly lit area. Why hadn't she left with the others? When the driver's window hummed down and she heard James's voice, relief raced through her body, performing cartwheels of exultation.

'Ally, you're just leaving? Get in, I'll take you home.'

It was so good to see him! Warmth cosseted her as she sat back on the sheepskin-lined seat. His face was shadowed and the street lamps did not reveal his eyes. She struggled for calm.

'I told you to leave at five-thirty! I don't like the idea of you going home alone in the dark.'

'Yesterday I left early. Today, just as well I had my alarm clock! You were going to work?'

'Briefly. I flew in half an hour ago.'

'Problems? You looked tired the other day. Carry on at this rate and it'll take forestry experts to count the rings under your eyes!' She could see his white teeth in his smile. 'Don't overdo it, James.'

'Listen to who's talking!' He touched a curl which swung like a loose spring. 'It's good to be with you. Though you've been very distracting!'

'Me? Why?' Delight bubbled at his admission.

'Because I keep thinking about you! Remembering! Though you're about as encouraging as a snapping crocodile.' He smiled. 'You're a danger to my plan. I have no intention of getting married for years. There's the business first.'

'So you see your future wife as a beautiful accessory to a successful man? An elegant, obliging sleeping partner, not an equal?'

'Get down from that high horse before you get bucked off!' He grinned. 'I want to marry a woman I love, who loves me. A balanced partnership. I'll enjoy cherishing her, having children ... but before I can think about the future, I must put my time and effort into the business.'

'Money!' she sighed. 'How much can you spend? How many houses can you live in? How many meals can you eat?'

'It doesn't work like that!'

'Doesn't it?'

A blanket of anger rolled between them. 'Look, Alice, I'm ambitious. I want to make Tasman's grow. If it doesn't, we won't be able to compete. Markets are tighter than before. I'm responsible for the livelihoods of my staff—many of them have been with our family for years. We've turned the corner, but there's a long route ahead. To me, it's an exciting challenge. Now, I'm going to collect some papers. Either you can come in for a couple of minutes or wait in the car.'

'I'll wait here.'

They'd done it again, Ally mourned as he slammed the car door, fighting each other with sharp verbal swords, yet she had been so happy to see him and he had appeared pleased to see her. Shoulders slumped, she recognised defeat. The differences between them were too deep. A relationship which led to conflict was not what she wanted. Should she leave while she could, maintain her emotional independence? In another ten minutes the bus would be at the stop round the corner. She scrabbled in her bag for paper to write him a note.

James returned just as she was trying to put it against the steering-wheel. 'I gather that's not a love letter,' he said.

'I'd decided to catch the bus.' Her voice was a whisper. 'It's easier than fighting you, James.' She leaned back, a desperate rearguard protection from his advance. Her heart was pounding, a drum rhythm warning, beating a retreat, but she was held by the seat and by the wry tenderness of his gaze.

The touch of his fingers along her cheek was gentle. She was aching for his kiss, but he continued to caress her, his four fingers sensitive, outlining her eyebrows, exploring her ears, following the jawbone line to her chin, reaching up to her mouth. With devastating care he traced the wide curve of her mouth, worrying her lower lip until she trembled, her body shaking. She felt the grip of his hands, the tilt of her chin, and then he kissed her, his lips a firm, warm pleasure pressing against hers, seeking, disturbing, enticing ... Sensations, aurora-like, dancing, flaring, rioting through her where he touched. Bemused by pleasure, she answered him with her own kiss, melding, wanting, giving. Yearning for him, she murmured his name, his kisses on her cheeks, her eyelids, her earlobes, and a soft moan of ecstasy escaped her.

'Yes, you're right!' James's voice was dark, roughened with passion. He gentled her back against the seat, his hand lifting stray curls. 'We don't need to make love in the car park!' His tone was ragged. 'I'll take you to my apartment.'

She realised he had misinterpreted her. Or had he? If she was honest wouldn't she admit that he was right? They wanted each other. Their kiss had been the most sensual experience of her life. She had been kissed before, but the comparison was like a meander beside a stream, whereas with James she had been swept away in a river, their desires carrying them perilously close to reaching the vastness of the ocean.

It was all happening too fast. She wasn't ready to love James. For her, a complete sexual relationship would be a total commitment; for James, moments of brief pleasure, a biological reaction. Eyes wide, lips full, she shook her head. 'No, James, it wouldn't work. We're too different.'

'Different but matched. Man and woman, two halves of a whole.' He touched her mouth with his finger again. 'Your kisses are dandelion wine, golden, sparkling and intoxicating...'

He bent to kiss her again, and she melted against him, unable to resist the overpowering sensual pleasure closeness gave. As his mouth met her hunger she reached out to hold him, slipping her arms between his coat and his shirt, enjoying the wide, hard breadth of his back, the bones of his vertebrae, faint knobbles leading up to the plane of his shoulders, his body so perfect, the wide shoulders and chest, the slim hips, long limbs, the firm muscles of his back tensing under her exploring fingers. He moved, and she protested, her fingers trapped by the movement and the tight fabric of his suit coat.

He smiled, contemplating her. 'I've caught you, my dazzling dandelion!'

Caught! Lured by the physical attraction, the striking looks. Trapped like her mother and grandmother!

'No!' She was panting, unable to speak more. Visions of making love to James flashed in her mind, mixed and overlaid with images of James with other women. She was a passing whim, a dandelion! He was more accustomed to orchids, tossing them aside when they no longer pleased him.

She shivered, remembering. A fight between her parents. Her father shouting that he couldn't resist picking the flowers. The hysterical accusations and the sobbing sounds of her mother's anguish. Her father saying they meant nothing. In the morning he was not there...her magical, laughing father. She had waited for him to return as he had done all the other times, not comprehending that he would never come back.

Ally trembled, the old stomach cramps and nausea flooding her. She could not look at James. 'I can't. You have a special relationship already. I saw you together at the coffee shop. She's exquisite.'

'All the women I take out are beautiful creatures.' He was teasing, his eyes glinting with humour. 'One of the perks of my work. I meet wonderful women. Of course I love them. They love me!'

Ally had overheard her father say similar things in the same laughing tone. She felt as if her whole gut was being clawed.

'You said you'd leave me alone!' She dredged up the excuse.

'Your eyes gave me permission.' He looked at her. 'Ally, I was wrong? You've gone white.'

Distressed, she knew she could not explain. James would not understand. How could she tell him about her father? About his infidelities, his desertion. A dizzying black engulfed her, a roaring in her ear, a sour taste in her mouth. Her stomach revolted. She was going to throw up! She couldn't... Not now... not in front of James!

Opening the door, she stumbled from the car, bending over to the gutter to dry-retch. Nothing came. Shivering, cold, she wiped her mouth with a tissue.

'Lean on me, Ally.' James put an arm around her waist, supporting her. He reached over and wiped wetness from under her eyes with an immaculate handkerchief.

'Sorry, James,' she whispered.

'You couldn't help it! Mind you, I wouldn't have found it easy to be magnanimous if you'd been sick in the car!' He was relaxed, trying to make her see humour in a miserable situation. He folded his handkerchief and dabbed at her chin. 'There. You look better now, Ally. You remind me of my sister's china doll, pale and fragile— and cold. Come on back to the car and I'll take you home. To your place. That is what you wanted, isn't it?'

She drew in a slow breath. 'Yes, James, I'm all right now.' All right! The words were facile, saying only the things she could say. Why couldn't she be open with him? Tell him they were too different, their attitudes to sex opposed. Since she had been eight years old she had decided she wasn't going to trust any man until she found one who was reliable. One who kept his promises.

James led her back to the car and tousled her hair. Miserable, Ally was grateful; driving the car kept him occupied. Staring ahead there was a void, blackness. Like her own emptiness. Throwing up after they had kissed was hardly the way to win a man! It was bound to have finished her attraction in James's eyes.

So why was she upset? Wasn't that exactly what she wanted?

CHAPTER SIX

IT WAS after ten when Ally slipped into Tasman's the next morning. A spring fashion parade was in progress, and as she slowed to watch she was almost bowled over by two small figures.

'Ally, Ally—Alice!'

'Lift me up, Ally!'

The rapturous greeting and the cuddles worked miracles of love.

'Both of you, at once, Greer?' Ally smiled. 'You've grown too big, Geoffrey! Good morning, Mrs Thwaites!'

'Ally, however you managed to shop with these two around, I don't know! I've tried to ring you several times in the mornings, but there's been no reply,' her ex-employer told her.

'Mum has a part-time job and I've been working here, painting a mural.' Ally hugged the children. 'I've missed you, but I've painted you and some of your toys on the wall.'

'Can we see them?' Greer tucked her hand in Ally's, claiming proprietorship. Ally looked at Mrs Thwaites.

'Take them! You couldn't give me twenty minutes, could you? I'm supposed to select a suit, but with these two it's impossible!'

Ally smiled, 'I know exactly what you mean. Of course I can.' Hadn't it been through the twins that she had met James? And the relationship had developed because he had returned Greer's rabbit and seen the sketch. And then she had fallen in love. She corrected herself. She had almost fallen in love with James. After last night's fiasco it was over. 'We'll be up on the top floor behind the offices and sick bay. Press the unmarked button on the lift.'

Accompanied by the twins, she led the way to her work and stood back to see the twins' reaction.

'Me! Geoffrey too!' Greer's chuckle was sunshine. 'And Mrs Rabbit!'

'Mr Kiwi!' Geoffrey chimed in.

'The big white rabbit looks like my red shoes man,' Greer added. 'See? New shoes!' She put one foot out for inspection, wobbling as she tried to stand on the other.

Ally jumped; she had forgotten the likeness. It had to be the first thing to repaint once the twins had been collected. As the children examined the drawing, she enjoyed their excitement at discovering more and more toys half hidden by ferns.

'Spooky old trees, but I'm not scared!' Geoffrey had followed one of the paths towards the shadowy bush, but his sudden flight towards the security of her legs reminded Ally that she had to redraw the area. She remembered Mr Tasman's invitation to study his bush. Perhaps it would help, and if she could take the twins too, they could all share in the fun. She made a mental note to ask their mother if they could have a picnic afternoon. Parting Geoffrey's hands from their grip on her knees, she led him to see some of the soft toys. Greer continued to be fascinated by the painting.

'Good morning, Ally. How are you feeling?'

An everyday greeting, yet James's smile warmed her, holding, caressing. After the first rush of joy she fought down the impulse to walk into his arms. The night had been torn by rusty memories of her parents' fights and the fresh barbs of James's words. Unable to sleep, she had lain wet-eyed until exhaustion had lulled her after three o'clock.

'I'm fine.' She pirouetted, hiding the effect of his smile. His almost cerulean blue eyes reflected a tenderness that threatened. She clutched for a distraction. 'You remember the twins?'

'How could I forget?'

'I met them downstairs. Their mother's looking at suits, so I'm guarding them for a few minutes.'

'The mural is working! Especially the white rabbit! I think most of the staff have sneaked up here for a viewing. The general consensus seems to find a certain resemblance hilarious.'

'You don't mind?'

'Who could object to being part of a masterpiece?' Again the smile lit his eyes, curving his sculptured mouth. 'But I don't want to feature in the next one! Having said that, I want you to reconsider the rabbit as a central character. In New Zealand they're a pasture-devouring menace. Is it possible to change it?'

'Of course! How about a dragon or a dinosaur?'

'You can do that? Great! Thanks, Ally.' He glanced down at his clipboard and checked off a note before he looked back at her. 'I want you to start on the proper site soon; we're short on time.'

'I'm not ready yet! The background is wrong, the spray technique needs more work, more time!'

'Stop worrying! Look at the fine leaf patterns you've managed with the sprayer. As to the design . . . the children's manageress is thrilled, Grandad's pleased, the shop designers are impressed. Chris Rudge from the art and advertising section will be with you tomorrow. I had hoped to spare you another artist, but for the moment, that's doubtful.'

Greer and Geoffrey had started to argue over the toy collection, and James stepped forward. Greer, recognising him, ran up, displaying her red shoes. He admired them and asked after Mrs Rabbit. When he left a minute

later, Ally decided Greer was likely to be his fan for life.
The small incident confirmed her opinion. James was
drawn to females like a moth to light, like a bee to a
flower. He couldn't help his attraction, it was part of
him. A relationship with him would be like trying to
keep a paddleless canoe afloat in rapids. Sooner or later
the canoe would smash itself to fragments on the rocks.
She shivered.

A woman's high heels tapped across the floor.

'Ally, thank you! I managed to find exactly what I
wanted!' Mrs Thwaites looked at the painting. 'This is
wonderful! Love the handsome rabbit! There's the twins
and their toys! What a deliciously spooky forest!'

'Too Gothic, I'm afraid!' laughed Ally. 'I've got to
re-draw that area. Mr Tasman invited me to study an
area of bush beside his beach house. I wondered if the
twins would like to have a picnic with me there, this
afternoon or tomorrow? You too, of course, if you're
free?'

'This afternoon would be wonderful. I'm going for
an interview at three o'clock—part-time office management. There's a lot of competition for the job; not
many positions fit in with kindergarten hours.' She pulled
a face. 'My husband and I needed a longer break.
Working together isn't helping us. We're sniping at each
other the whole time. I feel so damned angry!' She drew
a long breath, struggling to hold together. 'Now, let's
get this afternoon organised. I'll pick you up outside
here at two-fifteen, drive you and the children to the
spot, then after my interview I'll rejoin you. I'll pack
some drinks and afternoon tea.'

'Don't worry, I can buy some goodies from the cafeteria,' said Ally.

After they had said goodbye, the storage area seemed
quiet. Ally was disturbed by the knowledge that the
Thwaites were having difficulties, despite the coun-

selling. She had hoped that everything would right itself, the picture-book family remain intact. Instead, it seemed to have split apart.

Unable to concentrate on her painting, she left the gear untouched and walked slowly downstairs to the children's floor. Her mood began to lift as she noted the changes; most of the fittings were in place and the new play area defined. She inspected the wall. The background colours of the sky had been painted on to her instructions, the floor by the wall had been left uncovered, the new carpet to be fitted once her work was complete. She checked her measurements as a matter of routine, noting them on the back of her book. Still not settled, she went down to the cafeteria and purchased some sandwiches, raisins and fruit juice, and begged four paper mugs from the attendant. Remembering the children's enjoyment of gingerbread men, she walked along the street to a bakery and selected two small Hansel and Gretel houses and some richly decorated gingerbread men, reflecting that if they were left over Katie and Jonathan would not scorn enjoying them!

As it was nearly lunchtime, Ally sat in the square while she ate her sandwiches. Love and James seemed to be synonymous. How could she resist loving a man who had such a sense of humour that he could laugh at himself? A man compassionate when she had been sick? But how would she feel if James was unfaithful?

A sparrow waited by her feet and she threw it the last piece of her sandwich. Could she be like the sparrow, content to wait until the crumbs of love were tossed in her direction? Another sparrow, seeing the large scrap, flew in and commandeered the bread, dragging it away, only to lose it to a starling. The allegory was obvious.

Ally decided James should remain solely in the realm of employer and, as such, she should tell him that she was 'going bush', as his grandfather had suggested.

Carrying her packages with care, she stopped at the office and, seeing James's door shut, left her message with his secretary.

She made a fresh foreground sketch in her book, then began working with the sprayer. At two o'clock, she cleaned away her equipment, changed into jeans and top and redid her hair, then went down to the front of the shop.

'Ally—Ally Alice!'

Geoffrey's call was distinct and joyous, his brown eyes sparkled and his arms struggled futilely with the straps of his car seat. 'Stay there, I'm coming with you!' Ally clambered in, with a smile for Mrs Thwaites. 'Did I keep you waiting?'

'No, perfect timing.' Mrs Thwaites eased the car back into the traffic.

'Picnic, Ally!' crooned Greer. 'We haven't been on a picnic for ages and ages and ages.'

It took only a short time to drive to Beach Road and find the small cedar and stone beach house. Avoiding the building, they trekked past the drive towards the slight hill, Ally noting the occasional stubby manuka and ngaio gaining ground until they were beside a rocky outcrop which formed a demarcation between clearing and bush.

'Limestone! Don't fall down any rabbit holes, Alice.' Mrs Thwaites grinned as they climbed, arms full. 'There might be caves in the area.'

'I'll be watching! Here, the ngaio will give shade.' Ally put down her load. 'It's like the first day of summer!'

'Groundsheet first. Daddy says groundsheets stop the damp,' Greer instructed, the image spoiled by her in-adequacies in unfolding the heavy fabric. 'Geoffrey, you're not helping!'

'I is too!' Geoffrey, holding the distinctive bakery box, placed it with the care an art historian would use handling the Mona Lisa. 'Gingerbread men, Ally?' His expression was hopeful.

'My son's chances are probably better than mine!' Mrs Thwaites's smile twisted. 'I must go. Wish me luck!'

Ally and the twins walked down to the car to wave goodbye, then ran back uphill to the picnic spot.

'The gingerbread men might melt, Ally,' Geoffrey said anxiously. 'I haven't had a gingerbread man for a long time. Greer likes gingerbread men too.'

Ally laughed. 'All right.' She opened the box and handed the two biscuits out. 'The rest later, when your mother comes back.'

Eating a gingerbread man each required constant gleeful comparisons of icing shoes, socks and shorts and striped tops, but both left the smiling faces for the last bite. While they were so engrossed, Ally pulled out her sketchbook and began work. The lie of the land had already shown her how she could correct the mural by utilising a slope, rocks and scrubby manuka and ngaio trees to lead into the background forest. As the children, their gingerbread men disposed of, took a ball and began to explore the open slopes leading to the fenced-off road and beach, Ally pencilled in the sketch. Deciding that the twins were getting too close to the beach house, she called them back, but to her surprise they appeared to be talking to someone. She stood and began to move down the hill just as a tall, powerfully built, familiar figure came into view.

'James!' she exclaimed.

'Look at me! I can race you to Ally!' Geoffrey shouted as he scrambled past Greer.

'I'll beat you!' James allowed both children to win. Greer naturally swift, soon dived into Ally's arms and claimed a victor's kiss. Geoffrey expected the same.

'Me too!'

'Me three!' challenged James.

The kiss was thistledown on her lips, warming Ally with his gentle humour. Her heart was speeding and she had the feeling that James was aware of her body's joyous response to his arrival. 'I thought you'd be too busy to come,' she murmured, trying to appear blasé.

'How could I resist? I'd put the afternoon aside for assessing accounts and strategy planning, but one of the skills of management is knowing when and how to change plans!' His glance was a kiss that burnt. 'I won't even ask why you picked this spot. I bet Grandad suggested it!'

'You're right,' she told him. 'He said you should come too.'

'But you didn't want to ask me directly?'

'You're always so busy,' she prevaricated, knowing that his blue eyes were seeing her mental wriggles.

'Darling golden one, you and I are involved!' He ran his right index finger down her jawline. 'It's a question of trust.' He managed a wry smile. 'You've made a fan of Grandad! He's not easy to impress.'

'He's a remarkable man. I like him.' With an effort Ally picked up her book and pencil and checked the children. 'Would you entertain the twins? This sketch shouldn't take me long.'

'I'd rather amuse you!' His eyes sparkled and he leaned forward and kissed the skin revealed by the V of her blouse.

'I'm supposed to be working!' She flapped the book to ward off more teasing advances.

'Have I told you how fascinating you are? How your hair glints gold in the sunlight? How your lips are luscious strawberries of temptation?'

'Oh, please! No commercials!' she snorted with suppressed chuckles.

'Right, actions speak louder than words!'

Reading his intent to kiss her thoroughly, she plopped down on the grass. 'No, you don't! I'm working, Mr Bossman!'

'I'll find a more appreciative audience!' He blew her a kiss.

She watched as he ran towards the lower part of the hill where the twins were playing with a ball. Geoffrey, throwing the ball with a definite lack of co-ordination, was given a quick lesson on technique, and his later throws showed the improvement. James's praise worked chest-stretchings of pride, and Ally, looking up frequently from her drawing, was surprised by Geoffrey's rapid progress. Greer, who had the task of fetching the ball, had been observant, demonstrating her superior prowess when she threw the ball back to Geoffrey. James's praise brought more smiles to Greer's face. Before they could tire of their new achievement, James suggested racing to the top of the hill, and allowing them a lengthy start, he had to stretch to catch them. Their giggles and squeals as he picked one up under each arm as he passed, setting them down as king and queen of the castle on the rocky summit, were too much for Ally. 'I couldn't resist all the fun!' she admitted as she joined them. 'And I've worked out the design problem.'

'Race me, Ally!'

Geoffrey was off and Greer started almost as soon. As Greer was about to pass, Geoffrey turned, announcing, 'I won, I won!'

'You can't declare the finish line just when your sister is catching you,' James spoke with a firmness that caused the offender to pucker his lips and his cheeks to wobble. 'That's not fair! Now, both of you, when I say "Go," run to Ally. Go!'

A minute later both children were beaming up at her.

'Well done!' James clapped his approval. 'Would you like to see a magic cave?'

'Magic? With fairies?' Greer was wide-eyed.

'I can't guarantee the fairies. It's not easy to see them, but you could see their palaces, and if you're quiet you can see their lights sparkling, so you'll know they're about.' He looked at Ally. 'It's not far—in the bush, about ten minutes away. Quite safe. I wouldn't let you or the children get into difficulties.'

Reassured, Ally nodded. 'Sounds great!' She took Geoffrey's hand, smiling as he held his other hand out to his new hero. Greer was perched astride James's shoulders, being deposited back to the track, when the tunnel-forming trees swept close.

'It's down behind the trees.' James explained, 'When we go into the cave it will be dark, so we'll wait at the entrance to give our eyes time to adjust. Ally and I will hold on to you. If we're very quiet, the fairies might let us see their lights. If you make a wish, then it should come true.' He paused and made a theatrical flourish. 'But only if you can get out of the cave before the fairies hear you and switch their lights off.'

It was a story her father might have told, Ally reflected as James, after explaining that he'd be back, went ahead to check the path and the cave. His wave encouraged them to scramble down the bank, and he swung the twins down the last steep drop. Ignoring his open arms, Ally attempted to bypass his offer, looking instead for a fern to grasp.

'Miss Touch-me-not!'

She saw James's folding his arms as though to capture his own willingness to help her. The bank had slipped at some earlier time and the regrowth was too weak to take her weight. She moved further along, seeking a possible way down, knowing that James had jumped safely, but the cliff angled, forcing her upward. With her luck, if she jumped she'd sprain an ankle and James would have to carry her out.

'Give up, my darling!'

She nodded, noticing his leaping smile as he tried not to laugh. Leaning forward, she slid down into his arms. As he held her, Ally read the tender challenge in his eyes. He wanted to kiss her, but he was waiting for her, and, secure against him, she answered instinctively, reaching up and kissing his warm curving mouth. His response, lightning firing and melting her as he deepened the kiss, left her trembling.

'Welcome to Wonderland!' he murmured, then stooped to enter the cave.

As they followed, the darkness closed over them, but Ally was conscious of James waiting beside her, giving them time for their widening pupils to adjust. Gradually she began seeing more detail. It was a large cave set with small stalactites and stalagmites; a cream and shadowed limestone land of miniature castles and turrets, a world where gravity played topsy-turvy. Close by, water lapped out of sight. Ally, tightening her hold on Greer, checked to see that Geoffrey was held by James. The size of the cave surprised her; it was some distance to the rear where it shelved to disappear into the dark. Ally was guided forward by James as he led the way past the delicate formations, until they were in the centre looking up at a cathedral-like dome.

'It's Fairyland!'

It was Greer who whispered, excitement and wonder overcoming the warning to be quiet. The cave ceiling and walls were covered with a cobweb of a thousand lights, shimmering and sparkling. Looking around, Ally appreciated its spectacular beauty.

The cave was a secret protected by its owners and its hidden location. While the Tasman family were its guardians, the glow-worms were safe. Resting against James, she felt safe too. James's lips touched her head, his movement a reassurance. In the enchanting setting she acknowledged that she was in love with James. The thought was frightening. She wished she could trust him, she wished she could be open with her feelings with him, but he had the gift of charm like her father. Once James tired of her, he would move on, abandoning her. The remembered cramp and nausea began to threaten her.

Geoffrey, tugging at James's hand, gave an excuse to leave. Outside the daylight shocked. Ally persuaded herself that the feelings she had for James were as temporary and ephemeral as morning mist.

'I saw a fairy!' Greer's excitement was champagne. 'It landed on my hand!' She examined her fingers as though to make sure the vision had gone. 'It was tiny and it wore a shining brown cape embroidered with white circles on its wings!'

'It was a moth!' scorned Geoffrey.

'It was a fairy!'

Intervening before a skirmish of words became a battle, Ally had little time to notice that James had to struggle to find toeholds climbing up the bank, despite his athletic skill and long legs. Concentrating on lifting the twins up to him restored her stomach to normality. She allowed him to help her in turn, but took care in keeping her glance away from his. On her feet, she grasped Geoffrey as a protective cover.

'I wished for another gingerbread man and two Hansel and Gretel cakes,' beamed Geoffrey. 'One for me and one for Greer. What did you wish, James?'

'You're not meant to tell,' frowned Greer. 'It might not come true!'

'I'm going to make mine come true!' laughed James. 'I wished that a golden-haired princess would fall in love with me.'

'Do you know a princess?' Greer was impressed.

'The one I'm wanting is in disguise. No one knows, except me, that she's a princess.'

'Come on—your mother might be at the picnic spot wondering where we are!' Ally heard her words jar, but she set off, brisk-paced. Imagining herself in caricature, lips pressed, chin forward, hair corkscrewing behind her, the twins dangling, treading air as they tried to keep up, slowed her down. 'Sorry, James. Thank you for showing us the cave. I don't think I've ever seen anything so beautiful!' They were almost at the edge of the bush, and she released the twins, who ran ahead.

'I'd like to know what frightens you, my princess.' James's voice was gentle, but his hand on her arm was a restraint preventing her from moving forward.

'Me? Frightened?' She shook off his hand. 'I'd better make sure the twins are safe.' Speeding after them, she tried not to see the hurt on James's face. Guilt and anger confused her emotions, so it was a relief to see Mrs Thwaites climbing up the hill and the twins rushing to tell her about the cave. Ally began putting out the picnic food, pleased to have something to do. She was aware of James coming to a silent stop behind her, his presence forcing her to face him.

'I hope you like Hansel and Gretal cake.' The words choked her as she saw his expression. 'I hurt you.'

'Yes.'

'You ask for too much.' The words were a mumble.

'Because I don't enjoy crashing into the wall you've bricked up. Until it's demolished, we'll continue to hurt each other.'

Ally fiddled with the paper mugs, unable to answer.

'I'll get going. There's no point in my remaining.' James, with a wave for the children and their mother, strode back towards the beach house.

'My wish! I got my wish!' A gleeful Geoffrey running and jumping in eager delight distracted Ally, and, between sharing tiles of chocolate roof and panes of almost translucent toffee windows, James's departure was accepted. It was only when she was back at home that his comments and her own wishes returned to harass her. To avoid the thoughts she went off to the workroom with her sketchbook. Re-drawing and graphing the altered composition kept her occupied until fatigue drove her to bed.

At work the next morning Ally discovered that the scaffolding from her practice area had been removed. Frustrated in her attempt to set out the revamped drawing, she crossed the floor to James's suite.

'Looking for me?'

James, smiling at her, made every cell in her body dance. It was an effort to appear nonchalant.

'My equipment! It's all gone!'

'Downstairs! Is that the sketch?' He glanced at it briefly. 'Looks good! Grandad will be pleased.'

'But I . . .'

'You'll be fine.' His smile was playing tag with her heart. 'Was there anything else?'

Ally shook her head, then moved away, perturbed by the dismissal. Had the gentleness in his words been her overactive imagination? What had he expected of her? Or was it just a routine enquiry? On the children's floor she found the missing scaffolding already in place. The elder Mr Tasman was standing close by, talking to the foreman.

'Alice! You've completed the sketch?' Mr Tasman waved her to join him as the foreman returned to his task.

Ally handed over her book hesitantly. 'It's just rough. I thought I'd be able to complete it upstairs.'

'And lose the white rabbit!' Mr Tasman's mischievous smile made him look twenty years younger. 'It's one of the cleverest cartoons I've seen!' He studied the drawing. 'You're still working on the centre? If these are portraits of specific children, get written permission from their parents, for our files. Tell Personnel to fix up a fee. The lie of the land is familiar! I'm glad I suggested it.'

'I was tempted to draw in the cave James showed us.'

'James took you there?' The old man looked surprised. 'My son found it years ago when part of the bank slipped away. James was a toddler at the time. My Alice and he called it the Cave of Sparkling Castles and made up stories about magic. Lot of nonsense!' He blew his nose with vehemence. 'Well, you've work to do, and not much time to do it.'

Ally smiled. 'Thank you for telling me.' The mental picture of James as a little boy remained like a candle-glow as she began marking out the grid pattern. By the time she noticed the workmen returning after lunch, she doubted whether she could complete the scene by the date James had set. Much would depend on the artist he had promised. She opened her sandwiches, and stared in dismay at the sketch. Another artist would rubbish it. She had to remedy the central space. One-handed, she flicked to another page and sketched a daffy dragon.

'You're Ally Barrett? I'm Chris Rudge. Apologies for interrupting your lunch hour.'

'You mean five minutes! I've almost finished.' Ally looked up at the tall, thin young man and her smile widened as she noted the artistic sense revealed in his bronze and red sweatshirt and red trousers. Chris Rudge was a man who enjoyed colour! 'I've been sectioning the wall, it's such a large space. You can start drawing in outlines at the window end.' She released the sketch from the folder and handed it to him. Conscious that Chris was a professional, she dreaded hearing his criticism.

'This is great!' he exclaimed. 'Original and fun!'

'You like it?' She added, still nervous and defensive, 'I've got to change the centre figure.'

'The rabbit upstairs? I knew then why the boss had been singing your praises. You're talented!' He looked at her open page. 'A dragon?'

'Yes, I can't keep the dinosaur in scale. I thought it would be easy to fix... Any ideas?' she asked.

'You wanted a small dragon? Why not a...' He picked up a pencil and drew an appealing creature.

'A tuatara!' Ally nodded enthusiastically, appreciating that Chris had mimicked some of her stylistic patterns. 'Perfect—he's a native, a descendant of the dinosaurs, and he looks just like a mini-dragon.' She thought for a moment, then drew in a motorbike on which a second tuatara sat pillion, crash helmet decorated with spangled stars and flowers. Chris, laughing, drew a set of leathers on to the first tuatara.

By five o'clock Ally was happy with the afternoon's work. The central figures had been resolved, and she had gained a new friend. With Chris she was at ease, able to discuss art, movies and environmental issues, discovering much in common. When Chris found they lived a street away, he offered regular rides in his car. Ally, with the proviso that she contribute towards petrol, agreed, yet the decision made her ambivalent. It meant leaving at more usual times, and the possibility of rides with James would not arise. But wasn't that sensible? James was not the man for her. Why couldn't she fall for a man like Chris? He was considerate, thoughtful, fun and open. His confession that he was afraid of heights and the prospect of working on the top scaffold worried him had been natural. She had reassured him that she would manage, not even mentioning that the scaffold had to be raised again!

A southerly wind howling viciously as it carried rain and sleet greeted the next day, and Ally was glad of Chris's transport. At work she forgot the weather, concentrating on redrafting the four centre panels, shifting a pair of penguins to balance the composition. Chris made progress with the outlines, his professionalism evident in the rapidity and accuracy of his work. Two days later the outlines were complete except for the topmost trees. The scaffold would have to be altered for the work and, confident James would stop by, Ally had waited to ask him to arrange it. When James had not appeared, she sought the floor manageress to pass on her request. The thought that James might be avoiding the mural area was disturbing. Had he decided she was a waste of time?

The faster the mural was finished the better. Once it was completed there would be no need to see James; he would be too immersed in business to give her more than an occasional regretful thought. For herself, she would paint over the memory and given time the colours of ecstasy would fade.

CHAPTER SEVEN

ALLY, along with the rest of the family, was awake at dawn. Katie was due to leave on a field trip, and the preparations involved anxious shouts for equipment which had been shifted, loud wailing accusations, and the penetrating smell of burnt toast. Ally gave up on sleep. It was pleasant to think of James, wondering if he was awake and thinking of her. She grimaced and swung herself up. Bed encouraged rainbow dreams; it would be more sensible to start work as soon as the security system would let her electronic card open the staff door after seven-fifteen. Chris would not be in until ten as he had a dentist's appointment so she had an ideal opportunity to paint in the topmost trees, without making him feel inadequate.

It was a disappointment to find the scaffold planks had not been raised. Deciding she could shift them up herself, she angled, tipped and lugged two boards into position. They were heavy to shift and she knew she could balance on one width. She climbed up in triumph, but disappointment followed, as the ceiling was just out of reach. From her perch she had an eagle view over the floor, and her eyes sighted two thick timber offcuts by the carpenter's rubbish. If she added the new pieces they would make up for her lack of height!

With the offcuts positioned Ally could just reach, but the strain made her decide to outline and paint the smaller trees first. Working from the corner, where she had the additional security of the side-wall, was relatively easy, but she soon reached the position of the tallest

tree. Stepping on to the blocks, she stretched up and
spread her left fingertips against the wall to balance
herself, as she reached out with the brush. The strain on
her underarms and calves was immediate. Her arms
became heavy and because she could not move her feet
her balance had to be considered each time she reloaded
her brush with colour. It was even worse when she had
to paint the lighter hues at the top of the tree. She lowered
her brush for a moment to give her trembling, aching
arms and legs a reprieve. The needlelike leaves demanded fine strokes, but each one seemed to be pinning
itself into her flesh. The heat of the ceiling area dried
the paint almost instantly, but it was also making her
very hot.

Beginning again, she was conscious of overstrained
muscles and sinews as ropes of fire. Trying to ignore the
pain, she concentrated with determination on the detail
of the tree. Sweat gathered above her eyes, between her
breasts and along her backbone, and she turned to wipe
her forehead on her sleeve and wobbled dangerously.
Steadying, she finished stroking in the last leaf of the
highest section. Another small branch had to be completed, but she had to wipe her eyes and rest.

Pins and needles pricked and jabbed as she lowered
her arms, the elongated fibres and tendons burning. The
bliss of the relief made her forget the offcuts, and she
eased one leg to rub the other in an attempt to mute the
pain. Her balance veered, and she clutched at and
gripped the end piping of the scaffold. Conscious that
she had thoughtlessly endangered herself, she held on to
the rod, panting until she eased down to a seated position on the broad plank. She untied her neck palette,
then flexed her wrists.

The noise of someone climbing the scaffold made her
frown; the last thing she needed was company!

'Alice! What do you think you're playing at?'

James, standing on the lower board. Angry! Alice, not Ally! Her emotions jumped somersaults. 'I'm just taking a rest. Is something wrong?'

'Stop playing the innocent! You nearly fell—twice!' He reached out, seized the offcuts and threw them to the floor. The bang and clatter as they hit echoed like accusations. Sweeping her brushes and paints and palette into her bag, he swung it down. 'I want you off there now. Slowly! Carefully!'

It wasn't the place or the time to argue, Ally decided after one look at his face; lines creased above his dark eyebrows and his eyes blue glacier ice. Her stiffening muscles were clumsy as she clambered down to his level, then followed him to the floor. She winced at the crash of her equipment as he flung the bag at her feet.

'Do you know how high you were? If you'd fallen you could have been killed!'

She tried to break his anger by being flippant. 'I wouldn't do that to your new play area!' For a moment she saw his fury flash, but, controlling himself, he took a step back.

'Go to my office! I'll see you shortly.'

He strode away to the stairs before Ally could reply. She picked up her bag, and pulled a face when she saw the mess the wet paint had made. Moving slowly on her banana limbs, she took it over to the sink-room. James could wait. She needed to rest and he needed to cool down. No authority-crazed male was going to order her around like a naughty child!

After resting, Ally stripped off her overall, washed away the green dots which looked like diseased freckles on her face and arms and brushed her hair free. She used the lift to save her tingling muscles. James's secretary ushered her into his office.

James stood by his desk, formal, in control, and gestured her to a seat. She chose to stand.

'Alice, could you tell me why you took such a risk?'

His headmaster pose annoyed her. 'There was no piece of cake saying, "Eat me", to make me grow taller.'

'This isn't Wonderland, Alice,' he snapped, his face muscles tightening and the pulse in his throat beating double time. 'No one works at that height without training, a safety harness and supervision. As for the additional risks you took with those offcuts...!' He paused for a moment, wiping a hand over his eyes as though he could shut out the scene. 'Why? You weren't meant to go above the picture rail!'

'The trees have to be there. They balance the composition.'

'They weren't on your practice wall!'

'It wasn't finished, remember!' she argued. 'The graph shows the trees.'

'I didn't realise. Scale is deceptive.'

He was blaming himself because he had not foreseen the danger of her intent. Intrigued at seeing the responsible facet of James's nature, Ally could not protest. He had been frightened for her.

'James, I didn't mean to worry you. I've got excellent balance.' She moved round to him and nestled against him, feeling his anger and tenseness dissolve as she smiled up at him.

'I'm trying to tell you off!'

She let her smile widen, gazing up at him flirtatiously.

'You're an aggravating, annoying enchantress.' His lips twitched. 'If anything had happened to you...'

'Nothing did,' Ally hid a wince as he gathered her, 'except a little muscle strain. And stop pretending you'd care!' Remembering the previous days, she leaned back against his arms. 'You didn't send me a message or bother to see me.'

'You missed me?' he crowed. 'Good, because I thought about you so much.' He pulled her back by tightening his arms. 'I flew North on the early bird intending to be back at four, but winds closed Wellington airport. So I went to Waikanae, then on to our Palmerston North shop, stayed overnight and caught the direct flight back. Appointments kept me busy.' He put his right forefinger on the full curve of her lower lip. 'You'd already left when I went down to your floor.'

Happiness showered Ally like a firecracker sparkler. She gloated in the tenderness and desire in his smile. His kiss was gentle.

'Don't think you can escape the lecture! You gave me the fright of my life! I didn't dare climb the scaffold or risk anyone calling out to you until I knew you were off those offcuts. Any disturbance and you could have fallen . . . then, when you lost your balance . . . Ally!'

The fear in his eyes distressed her, and she slid her arms around him, snuggling her face against his broad chest. 'Hush! You should know dandelions can survive in precarious perches!'

'I know dandelions are invasive,' his words were a deep murmur, 'but until this morning I wasn't certain that you'd grown in my heart.'

She felt him raise her face by gently pushing his left hand under her chin, but already her lips were full and moist, wanting his touch. His blue eyes held such intensity that she closed her eyes as he lowered his mouth to hers. His kiss was hard, deep and possessive; she could hold nothing back from his intimate, searching demand. When he released her mouth, she was trembling, shaking from her core. He continued to support her, dropping kisses on her hair, her ear, her neck.

'Dandelion!' he whispered tenderly as he touched his lips to the palm of her left hand, then cupped her fingers over to seal it.

She was suddenly afraid. Could one kiss make so much difference? 'James?'

'The chemistry was there when we met. There's an affinity between us. Making love together is going to be sensational.'

She slipped out of his arms, unable to face the searchlight of his joy and her own fears. A quick break would hurt less than a lingering pain.

'I'm sorry—I shouldn't have let you kiss me like that. Or maybe it was me kissing you,' she added wretchedly. She could feel her cheeks burning and was glad her hair falling forward hid most of her face. 'I didn't know emotions could skyrocket like that. I don't want to have an affair with you.'

The buzzer of the intercom startled them, and the secretary's voice informed James of the arrival of an expected buyer.

James, swearing, moved back to his desk and pushed the slim button. 'Five minutes.' He released the switch, but his manner was businesslike. 'Ally, we have to discuss this further. I'll have an hour at six. If I meet you at the mural area, will you come with me to the apartment? We can talk there.'

Fear. Knife-sharp. Pretend, delay. Alone together, the pull of physical attraction could overwhelm. Ally wanted security, one special man for life... James was not the type. 'What? No invitation to view your etchings? Even your grandad can do better!' She managed a smile. 'Sorry, my turn to cook tea. You could come home with me, if you like.'

'But I'd have to share you with your family! And you'd probably feed me on a salad of nasturtiums with dandelion wine!' He wound tendrils of her hair around his fingers, then released the corkscrewing curls. 'I can't tonight. On a first occasion it would seem rude to eat and run. No insults intended.' His grin was wide. 'I've another engagement at eight. I'll see what I can arrange tomorrow. Before I forget, I went down to tell you the

Art Department can't spare anyone else. Personnel are working on it.'

So much for romance, Ally thought with some asperity. Hadn't she known that James could turn charm on and off as easily as she could turn a seam? 'Chris explained. My friend Anne starts three weeks' holiday tomorrow from her design course. Could she have the job? She's a better artist than I am. She's coming here to have lunch tomorrow.'

'Fine. Offer the artist's pay rate and fix it with Personnel.' James squiggled a note on his diary, then looked up at her.

His gaze disturbed the fragile cover over her emotions. If he kept looking at her she wouldn't be able to resist... he could see she wanted to be close to him. 'James, I can't... see you tomorrow. Or any time! Not if you want your mural finished! You threaten me, I find you too attractive...' She was gabbling, gasping, admitting too much.

'I threaten you?' James sounded incredulous, but he had moved away to the window and thrust his hands in his pockets. 'Ally, until you finish here, I'll treat you like any staff member, I did promise that, and I meant it. You'll have to come to me. But promise me that you won't take any more risks?'

Nodding agreement because her voice had no breath to shape into sound, Ally managed to leave the office, but she took recovery time in walking to the personnel section. Back at the mural area, she was relieved that Chris was busy with the sprayer, which meant she could work without her silence being remarked upon. She painted a monkey hanging at waist height so she could work sitting down, but by mid-afternoon she was exhausted.

'Chris, I'm giving up for the day,' she announced.

'Fair enough! Do you want me to run you home?'

'No, thanks. My bike's here and it's sunshine and blue skies out there. It'll be good to blow away the smell of paint.'

She tidied her equipment, said goodbye, then on impulse decided to take home some of the delectable specialities Tasman's offered for afternoon tea. Her mother and Jonathan would appreciate the gesture, and she could put Katie's aside. An after-school 'party' had long been a family way of celebrating. As she went into the coffee bar foyer, she saw James seated at a table in the corner. He was reaching out to take the hand of his companion, the beautiful blonde.

Alice turned and fled. By the time she reached her bike and dragged it from its stand, she had convinced herself that James's behaviour was predictable. Why had she presumed his relationship with the exquisite creature had finished? Hadn't he admitted that he loved beautiful women? How many other women thought he was the one and only man? How could she have been such a fool?

Biking gave her a physical release. The repetitive squeak of the front wheel did not penetrate until she reached the park by her home. She locked the bike to the park bench, then walked under the trees, her anger becoming sadness. She began to notice the abstract patterns, light and shade on the grass, made by the flickering shadows of sunlight striking the tall gum trees.

Ally crossed the empty football fields to one of her favourite haunts, a woodland area left unmown over winter. Naturalised bluebells, star ipheons, forget-me-nots, grape hyacinths were mauve-blue and white sweeps of carpet. Dandelions blazed amongst the grasses at the edge. They were unwelcome intruders, too bright for the delicacy of the misty pastel world a long-ago gardener had created.

James's name for her was appropriate! Her colourfulness had caught his attention, but he would make sure she would not infringe on his planned existence.

'Ally! The mural's going to look wonderful!'

Anne's sincerity was too obvious to doubt. 'Look at the monkey! I love the wicked glint in his eye! You can see he's thinking about pulling the tail of the superior Siamese cat! Here's the house of the Three Bears! They should look surprised—the man in bed looks nothing like Goldilocks!'

'You're right!' Ally was sure Anne and Chris would like each other. 'Come and meet him—his name's Chris Rudge.' She performed the introductions. 'Chris is going to lunch with us—back-up to help persuade you to come and work on the mural for the next three weeks. The pay's good!'

'You just mentioned the right word—money! I'm so broke!'

'You can start tomorrow morning!' Chris grinned as he led the way towards the stairs.

Talking amicably, they walked to the coffee bar. Ally could not prevent her quick inspection of the customers, but neither James nor his companion was there. Lunch was almost over when James walked into the foyer, saw them and approached. Ally introduced him with buttered smoothness, determined not to let the two observers at the table know her sudden emotional chaos.

'Anne of Alice and Anne, Artists!' James was smiling. 'According to Alice, you're the superior artist. I hope you can help us.'

Ally watched his charm melt level-headed Anne. Having established that Anne was able to begin work the next morning, he moved on.

'What a dream! He's even more good-looking than his photo.' Anne regarded his disappearing form. 'I'd

work for a few cents just to have the chance to know
him.'

'The boss has a marvellous appeal for women,' Chris
mourned. 'I wish I had half his charm.'

'There's a difference between charm and sincerity.'
Ally heard the fire in her voice and hastily changed the
subject. 'Anne, if I take you to Personnel, we can get
your forms fixed up. We often start early and work late.
You don't mind?'

'So long as the buses are running.'

'I'm the chauffeur. I could pick you up too,' Chris
volunteered.

Ally, pleased with her matchmaking, resisted imi-
tating the Cheshire Cat. After she had returned to the
mural she began work with the sprayer, suggesting to
Chris that he draw his tuataras in the centre panel. His
delight rewarded her.

Some time later she felt as if she was being watched.
She looked up. James, a few feet away, smiling at her.
The intimate, tender, glowing smile which told her he
enjoyed the simple pleasure of watching her. Deliberately
she turned back to her work. When he moved across and
spoke to Chris, sending him off on a message, she kept
painting. James reached across and switched the sprayer
off. Annoyed, she pulled off her headgear. 'You wanted
me?'

'Always! Ally, something's wrong, isn't it? At lunch
you were like a cat whose fur's been stroked the wrong
way. Stop glowering at me. I don't know why you're
angry.'

She had fooled her best friend and Chris, but James
had spent two minutes and sensed her rage.

'Yes, I am angry. Hurt too.' The lump in her throat
grew bigger, and she had to swallow before forcing out
the explanation. 'I saw you yesterday, in the coffee bar.'

'You should have joined us,' he said. 'Lena and I go back to kindergarten and beyond.'

'Was it necessary to look into her eyes? And hold her hand?' Ally's anguish made her sound like an accusing harpy.

James's eyebrows drew together, a thick black line. 'I was telling Lena about you—I wanted her to understand. Alice, if you and I are to have a relationship, there has to be trust. Think about it.'

Miserable, Ally watched as he strode back to the lift. Ramming her protective gear into place, she picked up the sprayer and snapped it on. Trust! James had told her little, and denied nothing. Conman-like, he had avoided discussing it, showing anger at her reaction, and implying that she was the one at fault. She had to trust him! Without knowing him, how could she trust him? His staff loved him, but they only speculated on his personal life. James managed to keep that private.

The mural was almost finished, but Ally was not sure of any answers. James appeared to be committed to running the Tasman shops, his time divided between senior training, management and trips to other branches both in New Zealand and Australia. His grandfather was a frequent visitor to the mural area, and Ally enjoyed his acerbic wit and his observations. Anne and Chris had seemed a pair from the beginning, their romance flowing as naturally as water downstream. The contrast with her relationship with James could hardly have been greater.

A gap yawned every day when she did not see him. James treated her with the courtesy he gave to his staff. When he stopped by the mural, her heartbeat sped, her muscles tensed and it took conscious effort to appear nonchalant or engrossed in her work. She knew he observed not only their progress but her appearance, from the gold curls leaking out from under her scarf to the bright socks on her trainer-clad feet. At times she saw desire in his eyes, but he made no suggestion for a date. The longest time they had chatted had been at the end of Anne's three weeks, when she had asked him if Anne could continue to be employed after lectures until the mural was finished.

Ally sighed and dipped the brush into the silver paint. The elephant's tap-shoes shaped up under her brush, and when the fourth one was completed she stepped back to appraise the effect. Her smile grew. The silver was the finishing touch and worth her insistence on a particular superior brand. Stepping forward, she began silvering a braid on the lion's waistcoat.

'Ally, you're here alone? Where's Chris?' James, frowning.

'The courier brought the silver just as we were leaving. I told him I could manage. Thanks for giving the supplier the hurry-up—I was afraid it wouldn't be here in time.' She could hear the false brightness in her tone and knew her breathing had quickened. How could she continue to be affected by James? She spoke briskly to mask her emotion. 'Can you change the time lock so I can stay later than seven-fifteen?'

'I'll be working. Just come to my office when you're ready to go.' His smile twisted. 'I remember the tap-dancing elephant you drew for Greer. I've sent the twins an invitation to the opening.'

'That was thoughtful. They're looking forward to it. Mrs Thwaites rang me.' She knotted the words together. 'I'd better carry on.' She turned back to the silvering, using the work to hide her emotions, yet she knew when he picked up the reports and walked to the stairway. When the doors had ceased swinging, her emotions were still unsettled.

Why should she feel sad, as if she was forcing James out of her life? Like a magic wand which could make her forget, she dipped the brush in the silver and concentrated her attention on the threadlike circles she was embroidering on the braid. Each had to be the same as the one before, and her work was meticulous. Completing the braid took her till seven o'clock, but the effect pleased her. On impulse she decided to add a similar touch to the ruffs of three lion cubs. While she was adjusting the light, she was alerted by the sound of the lift. Moments later the lift stopped at her floor and James stepped out holding a familiar box.

'Ally—pizza, salad and drinks. You must be hungry!'

The aroma of onions, melted cheese and spices intoxicated.

'Food! Smells great! I was just thinking I'd have to go home, but I wanted to finish the first ruff.' Ally wiped her brush as James ripped back the cardboard. She looked at her paint-stained hands. 'Don't touch it until I've washed up!'

'I can't wait that long,' he laughed. 'Come here!' He selected a piece of pizza, broke off a section and put it into her mouth. The closeness of his fingers near her lips was startlingly sensuous. She bit on the soft melted cheese and crust, every part of her vibrant. It took a controlled forcing of her will to avoid looking at him, before she turned and walked to the washroom.

James's gesture had been natural, so why was she trembling, a leaf blown in a hurricane?

On her return James had set the food ready. A gesture told her to help herself. 'The designers were in today. They're impressed with the mural, in fact they want your address. I believe they'll suggest your work with some of their other artists. One of them described your work as Pre-Raphaelite Disney.'

'Don't pull my leg!'

'I'm not! Even if you do have sexy legs.'

The torch in his blue eyes was lit by his smile, and she saw the James she loved. 'And you, James? Has it been worthwhile?' Her agony was restricted to brief flicks she had of him, walking on to the floor, hearing him talk to staff, his warm praise, his decisiveness, his attraction...

'Worthwhile... That's not the word I'd have chosen. Grandad said it would be a work of art, and I think he's right. The composition is balanced, the techniques are skilled, the colours interchange and blend...the subject matter's handled confidently, the artist has a sense of mischief and fun...isn't that the language of the critics?'

'You didn't answer my question?' Ally bit into a small green olive, and the salt taste puckered her mouth.

James pushed away his cleared plate. 'I didn't think you wanted to know my feelings. I've been waiting for you to come to me—to explain, Ally. But you just kept on painting...ignoring our feelings for each other. Every morning I think, Today, Ally will come to me... Every male in the place, from Grandad to the messenger, dotes on you; with them you're sunshine and laughter. With me, you withdraw. That hurt.' The skin around his eyes and mouth tightened as he looked at her. 'They don't dream of being your man. I do. Of making love to you, touching the sweet curves of your body. I've been observing you, trying to understand. You're gentle, spontaneous, warm-hearted. But you refuse to acknowledge the sexuality between us.'

Ally saw his frustration, anger and pain. Realisation that he had found it equally galling almost pushed her to telling him about her father and his abandonment. But just in time she remembered the exquisite Lena, who frequently lunched with James, and his escort of visiting glamorous models. He hadn't appeared to be suffering! Did she want an affair with a man who was a Casanova?

In the continued silence James stood. He dumped the remains of the supper into the rubbish bin and snapped the lid shut. His gesture seemed to include her.

'I usually work till ten. When you want to leave, just come up and I'll call you a taxi. Book it to Tasman's.'

Ally nodded; if she spoke her voice would crack with tears. When he walked away, her eyes kept misting, and she snuffled into her tissues. Why couldn't she explain?

She wanted to go home, throw herself on her bed and wallow in self-pity. But that meant going to James, and he would take one look at her reddened eyes, guess that he was the cause, and if he held her and kissed her she would have few defences. Her whole body was quivering, and she made herself walk up and down the length of the mural several times, until she was back in control. Beginning work again was the logical course, and she knew it would mute the pain. Her focus was so intense that she could shut out the thought of James.

An hour later she heard his footsteps on the stair and the swish of the double doors. He carried his briefcase.

'Ally, would you mind finishing now?' he said.

'Already?'

'I decided to leave early—can't concentrate. I'm sorry if that spoils your work timetable.'

'It's all right.' Ally straightened and massaged her wrist. 'By the way, don't forget the top branch; it's a source of temptation.'

'It's being done on Saturday.'

She nodded and began packing up, James helping her carry some equipment into the sinkroom. Working beside him, Ally was conscious of the sexual tension between them. In the mirror his regard caught hers.

'You're beautiful, Alice, even with silver in your hair.' He took the can from her trembling fingers. 'I was rough on you. I get angry with myself, with you. The past hour, I've sat up there, telling myself to forget you... that I haven't time to put into a relationship. But I look at you and I know you are my woman.' He played with a loose curl. 'I've tried to understand your rights too. But I find patience...' his hands slid lingeringly over her shoulders '...difficult.'

Ally kept her gaze down, trying to ignore the riot of emotions that danced and flared at his touch. She wanted his touch, wanted to feel his arms around her... She looked up at him from under her half-raised eyelids, meeting his blue eyes gentian-darkened by emotion.

Surprising her, James stepped back and moved to the door.

'You clean up in here. I'll fix out by the mural.'

Ally turned on the cold tap fully. Under the roaring pressure of the water she dunked the brushes, colour trails swirling and merging silver-white. James could have kissed her! What was he trying to do? Had it been a sincere attempt to apologise?

It took strength to turn the tap off to a drip and both hands to stop it. By the time she returned to the mural, James had stacked the rest of the equipment. As they walked to his car he outlined the plan for the weekend changeover.

'Official opening at noon Tuesday.' James started the car. 'You'll be no longer employed by Tasman's. I intend to take you out then.'

'That sounded more assertive than patient!' In the dim light she noted the strong outline of his neck, the shadow of regrowth darkening his beardline, the small twitch of his lower lip when he sensed her scrutiny. She loved the way his shoulder and arm muscles gathered and bunched, the movements hinted at under his jacket. So close to him, she was aware of his vigour, strength and confidence. His action in driving the car to the side and stopping it did not surprise her. She ached to kiss him.

'Your place, princess!'

Bemused, she realised he had opened his door and was moving round the car to open hers. The time gave her a few moments to squash her heated hormones into order.

'I'll see you tomorrow at work. Chris will pick you up?'

'Yes.' Piqued, Ally tossed back her hair. 'You're not jealous?'

'If I thought you were attracted to Chris he'd have been transferred!'

'You'd do that? But that's...'

'Abuse of power? All's fair in love, remember.' His smile cosseted, but he moved forward, escorting her up the path.

'And your grandfather thinks you're wonderful!' she snorted.

'Of course. He taught me!'

'With such a dubious character, I'm not even sure I should ask you in for supper!' she chuckled softly.

'Next time, dandelion. Goodnight.'

She stood at the open door as he ran back along the path. Her emotions were rollercoasting as she gazed after him. Why hadn't he kissed her? She frowned. Unless something was wrong? Had she eaten too much garlic on the pizza? Had poppyseed caught between her teeth? Grown a third eye? Or was it all some new game he was playing with her?

CHAPTER EIGHT

'...AND so I declare the first stage in Tasman's Mall open.' Broderick Tasman took the scissors and cut the ribbon holding the curtains in front of the shop names and the mural. The flash of cameras and the applause was followed by a tidal wave of people entering the new shops. Ally, beside James, caught his smile.

'Ally! Come on!' Greer and Geoffrey tugged her forward. Neither had any intention of allowing their places to be usurped. As Geoffrey, determined to be the first captain, climbed up the centre of a space ship, Greer was clambering on to the back of a wooden horse.

'Ally, the mural's brilliant!' the twins' mother admired. 'What will you do now? Good jobs are scarce. The last one didn't even send me a "Thank you for your application but..." letter.'

'That's rotten!' sympathised Ally. 'I'm not sure what I'll do.'

'If you're interested, one of my friends saw the twins' duvet covers and is hoping you'll design three for her children. She's quite prepared to pay—here's her phone number.'

'I'll give her a ring.' Ally pocketed the paper as James came towards her. Excitement made his eyes very blue.

'The twins are having fun! Thank you for bringing them, Mrs Thwaites. Ally, the photographers want you to pose beside the mural.'

'Do I have to, James?'

'Yes. Don't shake your head—all those curls besiege my male fantasies! You deserve acknowledgement. Chris

127

and Anne assisted, but it's definitely your work, Ally. Besides, Grandad would like it—more free publicity for the business. You look sensational, Ally.' James's voice was deep. 'I've never seen you in a suit before, and with your wonderful legs there's a case for suing for deprivation of mankind!'

Ally laughed and moved to distract his attention. 'Recognise the suit material? It's a silk and linen mix from Tasman's fabric department! I couldn't resist the gold colour, and I had the braid, so I decided to wear something more professional than painting gear today!'

'You made it? My bright designer dandelion! Which reminds me, did you meet the shop-design team this morning?'

She nodded affirmatively and slipped into place beside Anne and Chris. The photographers worked as she answered questions from the reporters, and, on her suggestion, Greer and Geoffrey were included and their photos taken beside their mother and the portraits. When the media had departed, Ally turned down an invitation to join Anne and Chris for lunch, knowing they had only a short time together before Anne's lectures resumed.

'My dear Alice, you look enchanting!' Broderick Tasman joined her. 'Thank you for the mural. A work of art! I've been watching the children enjoy it, and some of the more observant have been discovering the hidden animals.'

'I wanted to say goodbye to you, Mr Tasman——' Ally began.

'*Au revoir*! I have the feeling I'll see you before long!'

The children's shop manageress approached to speak to Mr Tasman, and Ally looked round for James. He was talking to a woman journalist, and, even from a few metres' distance, Ally could see the Tasman charm at work. Geoffrey waving to her gave an excuse to move back to the play area, and she tried to forget her sudden heaviness as she admired his skill. After the twins had left, clutching balloons and gifts, she walked back to the almost empty workroom at the side, to collect her gear and her pay cheque with its bonus and formal letter of acknowledgement from James. As she said her goodbyes to the staff, there was no sign of either Tasman, and the knowledge that James had not bothered with the courtesy of a farewell hurt.

Ally caught the bus to her home. For so long she had been desperate to finish the mural, yet, with its completion, she was deflated. So much for worrying about what she could say when James asked her out! She opened the newspaper she had bought at the bus stop. None of the situations vacant appealed and although her mother had checked on the employment offices for her, there had been little on offer in the past fortnight. While painting, she had been too busy to care, but, as the bus turned into her street, she decided job-hunting would have to be a priority.

Fingering in her purse for the ticket, she fastened on to the paper Mrs Thwaites had given her. Making three duvet covers would keep her occupied for a short time. How much would be a fair charge for her work? Two of Anne's friends had requested similar sets. Perhaps her mother was right... could it be possible to earn a living designing and making such articles? At Tasman's, listening to the discussions by the buyers at lunchtimes, she had heard that good quality lines at fair prices sold.

Could she sell to Tasman's? Her work would be professional, and if she could take orders it would be easy to personalise sets as she had done for the twins and Anne. The possibilities spilled fluidly, widening as she planned her needs. Already she had an industrial machine and an overlocker, and the old sleep-out had been turned into a sewing-room years ago. Fabrics were available at Tasman's. She knew nothing about costing and bookkeeping and advertising, but she could talk to James . . . She frowned. James worked long hours. Was it fair to run to him with her ideas and problems? He would instruct his Manchester buyer to order goods just to get her started!

Firming her lips, she made her decision not even to mention her proposal to James, until she was making money. She would make and sell without his favours! There were other shops, even the weekend market. The bus swerved to her stop and she climbed down, enthused by the possibilities.

If she made a few sets she would soon find the public demand. What could she lose? A couple of weeks, when she would probably be unemployed in any case? How many designs had she seen that she liked? Matched sets of sheets, pillowcases, valances and duvets were so expensive! She would have to do her sums; she had the receipts from the twins' sets which would give her a cost figure, then she would have to allow for her own designing, cutting and sewing time as wages, and add on tax. If she could earn a fair wage, she would be content.

By five o'clock she had discussed the plan with her family, checked her initial orders with the prospective customers, worked out the basic materials and planned a visit to Tasman's to buy stock. The bonus Tasman's had given her would cover her share of board for several weeks and enable her to buy her first supplies. When the phone rang, Ally answered absently, her mind sorting patterns and possibilities.

'Ally? James. I'm sorry I missed you earlier, I'll pick you up in half an hour, say five-forty? You're coming home with me. My mother suggested you might like to see some more of Grandmother's paintings and then have dinner with the family. We're celebrating a successful start to the mall, and I can make you bigheaded by passing on some of the praise I've heard about the mural.' His voice cosseted her.

'Thank you! I'll be ready!' As she put the phone down, joy and anxiety pulled her in alternate directions. She should have said No. James had ordered, not asked! Going to her bedroom, she wondered what to wear. Her wardrobe had lots of leggings and sweatshirts, but, apart from the yellow suit, little more formal attire. She pulled out a long brown skirt and riffled through her blouses, her fingers slowing as she selected a cream silk that had been one of her charity shop prized 'finds'. After a shower, she slipped into her prettiest undergarments and blowdried her hair. Twenty minutes later she viewed herself in the mirror; apart from her hair, she looked rather like a maiden from an earlier sepia photograph. Her hair, a mass of gold curls, was too modern in style, and she searched through the array of junk jewellery in her drawer until she found a comb she had decorated. Twisting some of her hair up, she anchored the roll with the comb, then checked in the mirror.

Footsteps along the path warned her that James was about to ring the bell. It was too late to change her outfit or her mind. She heard Katie and Jonathan arguing over who was to open the door and quickly beat them to it. The expression in James's eyes as he took in her appearance delighted her. She performed the introductions to her family, and, although her mother offered James a drink, was relieved he asked for a raincheck. Her mother had cautioned against any relationship with James Tasman, but although Ally understood she didn't want to think about the possibility of deceitful charm. She just wanted the warmth of James's smile, the knowledge that he was thinking about her, the pleasure of sitting beside him as he drove the vehicle past the city limits to the green of the countryside.

'Dandelion, I wanted to apologise about lunchtime,' he told her. 'A journalist arrived late and missed the opening, so I had to go through the media release. When I returned, you'd already left. I tried your home, but there was no reply. I decided to call you later, but I got tied up with some figures.'

'The remains of a two and an eight are clinging to you!'

'I prefer yours...' His voice was sensuous with laughter. 'Tantalising curves, rounded little buttocks, firm thighs, strong calves and perfect ankles. All that cycling! You wore open sandals the other day and I saw candy-pink nails on your toes. On your left pinky you have a...corn.' He grinned, slowed the car as they crested a hill and on the saddle he drove to the side and stopped.

'Did you have to mention the corn?'

'I was pleased to see it!'

She pulled a face. 'Believe me, it hurts at times!'

'Insurance! If you know your mythology, the gods used to carry off perfect young women. But I never read anything about them being jealous of a woman with a corn, so I think...' he looked around '...we're safe!' She couldn't resist his teasing and smiled, but when he leaned towards her she was wary. His fingers cupped her face with tenderness. 'Ally, you have such expressive eyes! I've longed for this moment!'

She wanted to reach forward and kiss him. The touch of his lips would be warm, the texture of his skin firm, his beardline faintly rough with the regrowth...the smell of him, warm musk tinged with lingering notes of pine and citrus aftershave...the clean freshness of soap on his hands. In the quiet she could hear the beat of her heart pounding out her need. Was her own sexuality going to trap her? The thought sobered her and she sat straighter in the seat, trying to ignore James's disappointment.

'It's so hard to keep my hands off you, when all I want is to love you. If I understood... What is it, my golden woman?'

Knowing he saw her distress made Ally want to confide in him. But would he understand? He had just spoken about myths; in one of the twins' fairy stories there had been a woodcut print showing the handsome prince cutting his way through thorn thickets to reach the princess. In the story the prince had the patience and skill to persist, but the modern man would dismiss her fears as 'hang-ups'. She risked a look at James and felt like burying her face against his chest and sobbing away her long-held grief. He was waiting for her, comforting as he played with a couple of curls which had escaped on to her shoulder. His sensitivity to her needs, and the conviction that he was the man for her, grew. But shouldn't she remember that for James charm was as easy to put on as his expensive business suit?

'It's all right, my Alice.'

Afraid to give way to her clamouring and circling emotions, Ally knew she had to move. She flapped one hand against the door until she hit the handle and opened the car door. As she climbed out, the wind was cool against her flushed skin. Walking along the roadside, she tried to analyse her feelings. Why was she so attracted to James? Why couldn't she accept his sincerity? She looked towards the car. James was outside, leaning against her door, prepared to wait. He was so big and rugged, the light on his glossy hair, the angles of his face shadowing his eyes.

Accepting his invitation had been a mistake. Yet she could not ask him to take her back to town; it would be rude to accept his family's invitation and *en route* change her mind. Instead, she could treat the evening as therapy; seeing James in his home would reveal their differences, make the barriers between them permanent. A stone weighted her stomach at the thought.

To stifle the disquiet she looked at the scene below them. The countryside looked like a patchwork quilt that had been tossed down, forming steep valleys and hills. She gestured to the landscape. 'Is there time for a walk? Just along the ridge?'

Together they walked along the line of the road until they reached the first corner. The silence between them had the hardness of diamonds, but Ally, conscious of the inevitable separation, could not speak. She flinched when James stopped her and put his arm around her shoulder.

'Alice, I want to touch you, to hold you. I'm a very physical man.'

Knowing she had hurt him, she reached up and put her hand against his cheek. 'James, it's not your fault.' She made a half-turn away, breaking the physical contact. 'I'm afraid...afraid of loving you.' Her neck bent at the weight of her head. 'Afraid of losing you.' She felt small and mean-spirited. 'You see, you shouldn't be interested in me at all. Really I'm not a nice person. I'm not brave and splendid. I'm just so scared...' She stopped, unable to babble more, as James lifted her chin so she had to look at him.

'Little one, hush!' He put both his arms around her, enfolding her. 'It's natural to be afraid—a caution sign warning of danger. But I won't allow anyone, not even you, to say things that put you down! Someone has damaged your self-esteem, and that affects your ability to receive love as well as give love. I want to help, Ally, but you have to trust me enough to tell me.'

She felt the swift touch of his lips, but she could not drag her gaze from the bitumen strip and the gravel pounded into the ochre clay along the shoulder edge of the roadside. How long had it taken to make the road?

Had the men who made it been faithful? 'A rolling stone gathers no moss'... 'Sticks and stones may break my bones'... but she had been hurt, and James was tearing away at the stone wall she had built. She couldn't explain, she couldn't let him see the cracks, she needed her protection.

'Ally, look over there.'

He had seen her agony, and the command as he placed his hands on her shoulders and turned her was a relief. She wondered if anyone else would be as patient.

'See the trees around the house, further along the valley? That's home.'

The slight pressure from his fingers reassured. He was not rejecting her.

'Ally, when I'm away, I always recall standing here. Coming from town, it's the first sight of home. My father used to start singing when he reached here.'

Ally tried to imagine an older man, like James, surrounded by a family, but the imagery was difficult. 'Tell me about him,' she said.

'Dad?' James's forehead developed two wrinkles. 'A child sees his parent from a particular perspective, rather like looking through a fishbowl lens, everything's magnified and centred round self... When I was very young, Dad was my own Superman! He could do everything and put right every situation. As I grew up, I found that he was ordinary, that he was sometimes tired and grumpy, that he made mistakes, that he was just a man. Somehow I loved him all the more. He was a lousy businessman but a great dad.' James smiled with a private memory. 'Physically, I take after him. He was tall, broad-shouldered, and his eyes were blue-grey like Grandma's. He was an only child, his parents had always been busy, so he made sure he gave us plenty of his time. We knew we were his world. He loved us. The business—well, it was part of his duty. He tried. I'm not sure if it was

because Grandad was such a dominating influence that
Dad never trusted his own business sense, or because he
preferred other things. Like golf! And swimming! And
football! Mum and he used to play a mean game of
tennis. They used to take us hiking up those mountains...' he pointed to the purpling backdrop. 'We had
great times, camping out, making a fire... Dad was a
rotten chef!' James paused for a moment. 'I miss him.
I wish he could have met you, Dandelion.'

'He sounds like a good man,' Ally said, unconscious
of her own wistfulness. She wondered how much was a
child's view of a parent and how much was reality. Would
such a paragon have been faithful? The thought made
her realise what a cynic she had become. 'You were
lucky.'

'Can you tell me about your father?'

His left hand was around her, but his gaze was on the
distant hills.

'I used to think he was a magic prince.' She looked
into the past, seeing her father again. 'Like his stories.
He was tall, golden-haired, with a mane of curls. Brown
puppy eyes which could make you happy or sad.' She
stopped, unsure if she could complete the picture. 'His
voice could carry the music of merriment or the rage
and splintered ice of Antarctic seas.' She was shivering...

'He... molested you?'

'No.' Surprised by the question, she looked at James,
his understanding helping her to examine her feelings
without the tearing nausea. 'At least, not physically.
Emotionally perhaps, but it was not intentional. He never
bothered about truth, if fantasy suited. A troubadour.
He should have been born in the times of travelling min-
strels. He was good-looking, charming, a rogue, he lived
in his stories. I loved him. Now, I think he was totally
selfish and cruel. Fidelity meant nothing. He'd disappear for days at a time, then reappear as if nothing

had happened. Several times Mother and I saw him with other women—he'd told them he was divorced. Another time he pretended that he didn't know my mother...'

She was a child again, lost in the agony of the past. 'There were rows...they'd scream at each other, then he'd swear he loved us. When my mother told him she was pregnant with Katie, he just walked away.' Ally, struggling with the hurt, made an effort. 'The demanding reality of his marriage and three children was something he couldn't face.' Her voice cracked and she gulped, sobbing the words. 'He never came back...yet he had promised me he'd always come back. He said he loved us, but he didn't...I wouldn't know if he was alive or dead.'

She was crying, noisily, the anguish pouring out like pus from an incised abscess. Gradually, she snuffled to an awareness of the comfort in James's arms, his hands stroking her back and the compassion in his face. 'Oh, James, I'm sorry. I shouldn't have offloaded all that on to you,' she moaned, trying to wipe her eyes and sniffing inelegantly at the same time. 'I never cried about him before.'

'Time you did. You've carried those hurts too long.'

'The front of your shirt's all wet and your tie's damp.' She mopped ineffectually at his chest with the large handkerchief she had screwed up, then realised it too was sodden. She found herself smiling at James's chuckle. 'Your handkerchief too.'

'I wouldn't have minded if I'd ended up swimming in Alice's pool, if it helped you, my darling.' They started moving towards the car. 'If you can accept that your father was the one with the problem, that perhaps he was afraid to love, afraid of his responsibility, for whatever reason, you'll help the past to heal. You can afford to be generous—your father must have been tormented every time he looked in a mirror. Always he would have seen shadows of your mother, and Jonathan and Katie and you.'

Ally was stunned by James's perception. She had accepted that the fault was in herself, her family. But her mother was wonderful and who could resist loving Jonathan as a wee boy? Photos of herself showed a tot with big brown eyes, a lively grin and tight golden curls. Laughing, placid Katie hadn't even been born.

'I never thought of it like that before,' she said thoughtfully. 'I always felt that I wasn't worth loving. As I grew up, I regarded all good-looking, charming men as selfish, deceitful monsters. I never trusted any male or allowed them to get close to me.'

'You're saying you haven't slept with a man?'

'I decided to wait until I found someone I could trust, someone who would be faithful.'

'Life doesn't come with guarantees! I've noticed that sometimes we're made to face up to our greatest fears.' He stooped to pick several bright golden flowers from the weeds by the road's verge. 'Darling, I believe now you'll be able to give a man your love.' He presented her with the flowers. 'I want to be that man. I love you, my brave, bright dandelion.'

Ally smiled back at him. With the bouquet of dandelions in her hand she reached forward to kiss him, like a bride, formal, offering a dedication.

'My darling Ally...'

She heard him whisper her name as he pulled her more closely into the circle of his arms. Her body was quivering as he began lifting tendrils of hair from the nape of her neck, and the thrills spread as he placed kiss upon kiss along her hairline to her ear, his breath sending erotic messages. Her lips were shaped to his, she was a wild woman, greedy for him.

'My little wanton,' he murmured. 'You're so passionate, making love with you is going to be...'

'A steamy affair?' Ally managed weakly, seeing the steam rising from his damp shirt. She took his right hand and kissed it. 'I'd like to ask you to help me. Can you be patient a little longer? Sex to me is a total giving of each other in love. I've always thought that falling in love would be gradual, that I would know my man, before we slept together. That love and marriage would go together. Have I been unrealistic?'

'Some would say yes, others would say no. But this is between us, just the two of us. If you need more time, it's yours. If your question is, "Am I ready to commit myself to you for life?" then the answer is yes.'

'How can you be so sure? We hardly know each other! I don't know what you think about basic things—family, religion, life, death, attitudes. You don't know me! I might be a streetwalker, a thief, a great pretender!' She caught her breath at the tenderness in his eyes and the certainty in his face.

'Alice, I was hooked the moment I saw you. I've watched you for weeks, and my feelings have deepened every day. You're my joy. I've never felt this way about anyone else. When you were jealous of Lena, I was angry that you didn't know me better. Now I know about your father I can understand. I'm going to be your husband, and we're going to be faithful to each other. Eternity's just about long enough for me to discover ways of loving you.'

'James, you must be the most wonderful man in the world!'

'Hold that thought!' His blue eyes were alight with humour and love. 'I might need to be reminded!' His kiss was possessive. She nestled in his arms, loving the feel of her big man, and her fingers against his skin explored, at first shyly, then more confidently. With his kisses deepening and demanding, she was losing herself

in the colours of ecstasy. It was a shock when James
groaned, as he gently pushed her to arm's length.

'Ally, I wish I hadn't given my word to wait. I've never
known such temptation!'

'I'm happy to tell you that you're not only marvellous
but noble and patient.' Her fingers curved around him,
reluctant to release him. 'I forget everything when you
kiss me. Being with you is so deliciously intimate—I
hadn't realised a man's body could be quite so magnificent. It's going to be fun getting to know yours.' She
paused at a sudden thought. 'I don't even know if you
have any corns.'

He roared with laughter, an open shout of happiness.
Ally was picked up and swung high so that her blouse
and camisole flapped over his face. He blew a raspberry
on the bare skin on her midriff and lowered her to the
ground. They were standing, looking into each other's
eyes, when the sound of an approaching car broke them
apart. Instinctively Ally smoothed her clothes.

'It's Grandad,' said James.

They waved and received a toot on the horn as he
drove past. James put his left arm around her shoulder.
'I'm pleased you and Grandad get on so well—he's very
special to me. Come on, my dandelion, time to go.'

In the car she repaired her make-up, combed and re-
pinned her hair into place, conscious of James watching
her.

'You have the most glorious hair, my darling Ally. A
veil of gold curls. Very sensuous,' he added, then, with
a show of reluctance that made Ally smile, he started
the car.

As they drove down the hill and entered the valley she
glimpsed the homestead, a picture-postcard view, surrounded by its protective plantings and trees. As they
turned into the driveway she was impressed by the style
of the house. Its simplicity of line appealed, the pro-

portions balanced, the harmony created between landscape and house natural. 'It's perfect!' she breathed.
'Oh, James, for the first time in my life I know what
envy means!'

'Welcome home, my Alice!' James stopped beside his
grandfather's limousine. Ally was suddenly uncertain.
It was all too far away from her own lifestyle. The
mansion, the groomed lawns and gardens, the luxury
cars...

'Come in!' James had come round to open her door
and help her out. She stood silent, eyes wide. There was
the gentle pressure of his lips as he kissed her quickly,
then his lips searched and found her chin, her cheek,
her eyes, her left earlobe, then returned to her mouth,
and his hands slipping lower down her back sent a rush
of pleasure through her.

'You would start seducing me in front of every window
in the house, Ally! What's my mother going to think?'

His comprehension and mockery restored her. Life was
going to be joyful because the man she loved also loved
her and was sensitive to her feelings. Her throat
constricted.

'Don't you cry, beloved, I haven't another dry
handkerchief, unless I take you to my rooms, and that
really would put my mother in a temper! She has some
decided views.'

'What is James telling you about my views and
temper?' A tall, brown-haired woman with blue eyes
smiled a welcome. 'I can't say don't believe it...my son
always tells the truth! But I will add that his temper is
worse! You must be Alice Barrett—you're very welcome.'

The thunder of hoofs racing up the parklike area interrupted them. Two young riders bent jockey-like, each
struggling to outdo the other. With exultant whoops they
pulled the panting chestnut horses up on the edge of the
gravel, each claiming victory as they greeted their brother.

Ally was introduced, and she smiled at their easy affection.

'Do you enjoy riding, Ally?' Mrs Tasman asked as the younger two rode off.

'I don't know, I've never tried,' Ally admitted. If she had said she had never tasted bread, she doubted if the shocked silence would have been as obvious. She remembered her original impressions of James. Why hadn't she trusted her instinct? How could his world be hers? She was homespun cotton against his velvet.

CHAPTER NINE

'JAMES must teach you!' Mrs Tasman said reassuringly. 'Come in, Ally. I understand you're an admirer of Alice Tasman's paintings. While James changes, perhaps you'd like to see the work she displayed in the house.'

As her hostess spoke, she led the way up the wide steps to an ornately carved door and surround. Inside, a rimu-floored foyer opened on to a hall which in turn revealed several doorways and a curving staircase leading to an upper gallery. After blowing her a kiss, James took the stairs two at a time, and Ally followed his mother.

Mrs Tasman opened a door. 'Here's Alice's room.' They walked into a formal reception-room. Set against the polished honey-amber glow of the timber floor, the classic lines of the hall table and chairs were enriched by the dazzling colour of four wall-to-wall, floor-to-ceiling paintings.

'I've never seen such a room! Everything is so simple, so right... The paintings are...' Ally gave up trying to explain. If she said she was drowning in colour, her visual sense overwhelmed by the intensity and depth of sensation, it negated the soaring emotion and happiness in the large works.

'Come back, my dandelion!'

She turned to see James, realised they were alone and ran to him. 'I didn't hear your mother go out or you come in. I'm drunk with colour. This is love painted!' She kissed James, revelling in the closeness of him. 'I like the scent of your aftershave and body lotion.'

'Your perfume is a pleasant change from paint!' His eyes danced. 'Do you know how much you're teasing me?'

'No!' she laughed. 'But I'm just copying some of the brush-strokes used in the paintings. It's this room—it's full of exploding colour.'

'One day we'll make love in here.' He gestured with one hand to the walls. 'I used to call these abstracts Grandma's happy pictures! But my favourite is in Grandad's suite. He's there now, if you'd like to see *The Dandelions*.'

'Of course I would!' Ally reluctantly stood apart. 'You look enticingly sexy with your hair all damp from the shower.'

'Good! Because the woman I'm trying to impress is so beautiful, I need all the props I can get!'

'You think I'm beautiful?' Suddenly she wanted to be beautiful in his eyes. It was a startling thought. Almost shy, she looked at James and melted at his expression.

'Only you could be so unconscious of how beautiful you are!'

Dizzy with happiness, Ally floated beside him up the stairs. At the top, a pedestal vase of leaves and flowers looked like the gathered essences of spring. It was the type of arrangement her mother would prepare for the cathedral or a stage set. Further along the gallery was a cabinet displaying a large collection of netsuke. James didn't even glance at its treasures. Dismay began dimming her joy. The house was James Tasman's background but it wasn't hers. He led her along the gallery and ushered her into a sitting-room. Broderick Tasman looked up from his newspaper and stood up.

'My dear Alice—a Pre-Raphaelite goddess! You came to see *The Dandelions*?' He waved towards the picture above the fireplace.

'Thank you, Mr Tasman. Your home is impressive.' Ally studied the small picture. 'It's delightful! A posy of dandelions dropped on the grass.' She chuckled. 'Look at the fairy clock! If I blew it, the tiny parachutes would fly! The artist must have used one hair for the brush!' she admired.

Broderick Tasman looked out of the window. 'My solicitor has just arrived,' he said. 'We'd better go down.'

With James and his grandfather, Ally moved towards the gallery. From there she could see and hear the warm greeting of Mrs Tasman and the tall, blonde figure in the doorway. As they reached the lower steps, James walked forward and gave the newcomer an affectionate kiss.

'Lena—what a pleasant surprise! You look ravishing! Come and meet Alice Barrett. Ally is the artist responsible for the mural. Ally, I'd like to introduce you to a dear friend, Lena Smithson. Lena has just taken over from her father as Grandad's solicitor.'

From depths of courtesy, Ally reached for the conventional phrases. Close up, Lena was exquisite, with wide-set blue eyes, smooth unblemished skin, long blonde hair bound into a chignon. Gold earrings set with aquamarines matched the pale blue silk suit she wore with the natural elegance of a tall figure. The arrival of the two younger members of the family, and their casual acceptance of Lena's presence, made Ally aware of being the outsider. Lena, one arm hooked through James's, the other holding a leather briefcase, was confident of her place. She was the perfect mate for James, Ally recognised in despair. As though hearing her troubled thoughts, James came to her side as they moved into the reception-room.

'Grandad looks as cocky as a full-feathered rooster,' he murmured. 'He's up to something!'

'This is an important day for the Tasman family,' began the senior Tasman, 'with the successful start of the mall changeover and the unveiling of the spectacular mural. Now, James, I've got a surprise for you. Tonight you become the proprietor of the five Tasman department stores in the South Island and the three Tasman stores in Sydney. I expect you to keep assisting me with the rest, but I'm giving you these now, as a mark of my faith in your business acumen and because I'm proud of you. Lena, the documents.'

Ally saw the surprise, delight and pleasure play on James's face as he watched his grandfather sign the papers. When it was James's turn he glanced up, and his smile included her. The applause and the popping of champagne corks told her that to everyone except James and herself, the news had been expected. James's success toasted, they gradually moved from the reception-room to the dining-room. The splendour of the room, the large antique table and matching, heavily carved chairs contrasted with Ally's own family's kitchen. The Tasmans' magnificent soup tureen alone would have cost more than all the china in the Barretts' kitchen. There was some satisfaction in deciding her mother's soup tasted better!

Making an effort, Ally joined in the conversation, and was enjoying herself, until Lena asked her opinion on the opera which had been staged earlier in the city.

'I'm sorry, I didn't go to it,' Ally admitted.

'You missed it? James and I love going to the opera, although we argue about which production we prefer.'

'Alice has been working late on the mural. It had to be completed in time,' James put in.

'Of course! The mural is a trip into a fantasy, Alice. Quite splendid. The hidden animals are so cleverly executed.'

Ally was dismally conscious that James had covered for her and Lena had charmingly diverted attention from

her lack. During the dessert, she noticed the heavily en-
graved silver spoons. It was all too rich!

Somehow she managed to make the correct responses,
but when the party moved to the adjacent living-room,
she sat on one of the slender chairs rather than the
comfortable sofas and pretended not to see James's brow
mark into lines. When Lena walked to the piano and
asked James to turn the pages for her, Ally was hurt
again. She liked music, but there had never been a chance
to learn an instrument. Lena played with confident grace.
As the music surrounded them, Ally decided that she
had no choice. If she loved James, she had to give him
up. She had nothing in common with his background,
education, or the world of retailing. She couldn't allow
him to make such a mistake!

She sensed his regard and wondered how to face the
next few hours. When he signalled to Jonathan to take
his position by the pianist, and then crossed to her, she
was defensive.

'What's wrong, my dandelion?'

'Nothing. Everything's quite perfect.'

'Come with me. We're going for a walk.'

She frowned and pointed to the musician, but James
shook his head.

'I've been polite all evening. Now you, my darling,
are lying to me—the first time and the last time. Clear?
So I either kiss the truth out of you in front of my family,
or we walk sedately in the garden and you can tell me
what's worrying you.'

The look on his face convinced her, and she took the
advantage of the end of the piece to excuse herself. James
opened the French doors for her and they meandered
on to the terrace and from there to the daffodil garden.
The fragrance of the blooms was heady. In silence, they
turned the corner, and Ally saw a silver swimming-pool.

'Ally?'

'Your home is even more beautiful by moonlight, James.' She paused, reluctant to hurt him.

'This is where I want to cherish you, beloved. I want to share it with you and our children...'

Ally could not resist as he drew her closer, his hands slipping to her waist, his head bending to meet hers. She wound her arms around him, her lips passion-shaped to his touch.

'My dandelion! This is the happiest night of my life. I found the key to unlock your love. I can hardly believe how lucky I am. You being here to share Grandad's surprise with me was a bonus. It's going to mean more work, but with you beside me...' he kissed her quickly as his fingers released the comb holding her hair '...we can fly to the stars! What would you like, my golden one? Tell me your dreams... I want to shower you with love. Tomorrow I'll order the family jeweller to make up a small dandelion on a pendant, enamel on gold, I think...' he leaned over and kissed the base of her throat '...and it will sit just there.'

'James! James!'

James swore softly as his brother called out. 'There are times when young brothers...'

Ally put her hand to her hair, repinning it into place.

'James—we need you! Lena's hurt!'

'Over here, Jonathan! What's happened?'

'Nothing much!' Jonathan sauntered up to them. 'But Lena's making it the big drama. I dropped the piano lid on her hand. It wasn't that bad... but she wants to go home, and she says she can't possibly drive herself. I did offer.' Jonathan grinned. 'Pity I haven't my licence.'

'You'll be old enough soon!' One arm around Ally, James guided them back inside. 'Now let's see, Ally, if I take Lena home, then come back for you...'

'I have a proposition.' Broderick Tasman was already shrugging himself into his coat. 'Lena lives on the road back to town, so she can come with me. I'm going past her door. Ally has to return to her home in town. Ally is a capable driver, she can drive Lena's car to the Smithsons' place, then join me as company. Any objections?'

'Yes, Grandad! You get to take two beautiful women home!' James was laughing.

'So I do!'

Ally watching the two tall figures hug each other, realised Broderick Tasman had taken control. For some reason he wanted the chance to talk to her. She noticed James's reassuring smile. Whatever Broderick Tasman had in mind, James was confident she could handle it. Lena, apologising for spoiling the evening, gave Ally the keys to her car. Ally thanked her hostess and said goodbye to the family, stopping to give James a lightning kiss.

Moments later, she drove Lena's car down the long driveway and headed back along the road, following the red tail-lights of Broderick Tasman's car. Nine miles further on, the lead car manoeuvred into another drive and Lena, stepping out, gestured Ally to the garage. After parking the car, Ally said a brief goodbye as she returned the keys, then took her place next to Broderick Tasman.

'Well, Alice, an interesting evening,' Mr Tasman drove competently, 'and your pleasant company back to town! A chance to talk freely. I must say I'm pleased with events. Tonight, when James brought you up to my suite, I could see you both glowing with love. It made an old man quite sentimental!'

'James is an exceptional man,' Ally said slowly. She made her decision to take James's grandfather into her confidence. 'I love him, but it won't work. In the end, I'll make him unhappy.'

'Can you tell me why you say that?'

'It's the differences... I've been kidding myself. James is polished, sophisticated. He's a professional man, university educated. Now he's a multi-millionaire! What can I offer him?'

Broderick Tasman laughed. 'My dear Alice, you are a modest little flower! I have respect for you, and that's something I don't have for many people. You're kind, thoughtful, perceptive, intelligent, unselfish, and virtuous.'

'Mr Tasman, you mustn't flatter me! You don't know me very well!'

'Perhaps I'd better admit that I've made it my business to do just that. A man in my position has to protect his family. Since my son died, James has become vulnerable, so I ordered his friends checked as a matter of routine.'

'Checked? You mean investigated? Trench-coats and dark glasses? That's disgusting!'

'Computers are far more informative. If necessary, I have the security staff. My grandson has always liked women, but until he met you they were butterflies. He talks about you to me, something he's never done about any other woman. James is like me in some ways. When I met my Alice, that was it. With her love I built an empire, without her, I wouldn't have cared.' He took a moment to gather his memories. 'Ally, in the circumstances, I think it's right to tell you that in your case, I ordered a further in-depth report—family, social, medical, scholastic, occupational.' Broderick Tasman pulled the car to the side.

'You invaded my privacy?' Ally exploded. 'And my family's!'

'Your life is an open book. You have a remarkable woman for your mother. I admire her strength and the values she implanted.'

Curiosity overcame anger. 'Just what did you find out?'

'Your father abandoned your mother before Katie was born. She moved here, bought the cottage and raised the three of you. Life hasn't been easy. Now, Alice Joy, your school reports were excellent, your teachers regarded you highly. They wanted you to attend art school—your marks were in the top ten per cent for art, but you turned it down because it meant years in training, plus the cost of fees and the equipment. You became a nanny and you paid for the training course yourself, doing outwork, making tracksuits. The manufacturer reported your work as proficient and regular...'

'Then surely, Mr Tasman, you can see the difference between James's world and mine? James needs someone well educated, sophisticated...like Lena.' The name was hard to say aloud.

'Heaven forbid! Lena would sleep with me if she thought it was worth her while! Now I've shocked you! I'm sorry, my dear Alice. Lena's clever, and her charm is considerable, when it suits. Even as a child, she was a selfish, manipulative monkey. I'm not sure I was wise in allowing her to take over as my lawyer when her father retired.' Broderick Tasman gave a mischievous wink. 'I told you I was sentimental!'

'I don't know what to say.'

'Then say nothing! Stop thinking rubbish about not being good enough for James. People are more important than possessions. The essential quality you already possess, a loving heart.'

Joy began growing and flowering as she considered Mr Tasman's words. She turned and gave him a radiant smile. 'Thank you.'

The faded blue eyes twinkled, then sobered. 'However, I had another reason to explain my investigation, because I turned up some information I believe you and your family should know. It concerns your father.'

'We haven't heard from him for years...'

'Your father kept moving, from New Zealand to Australia to Canada to the United States. For the last three years of his life he gained some employment as a freelance scriptwriter. Yes, my dear, he's dead. Three weeks ago.'

Somehow the knowledge that her father was dead seemed unreal. 'Thank you for telling me. Do you know what happened?' she asked.

'He'd been in poor health for some time. I faxed your mother's name and address to his attorney and she'll be sent the details. I think it would be better to tell her before the letter arrives. Now I'd better take you home.'

Ally was glad Mr Tasman concentrated on his driving. The night quiet gave her time to struggle with her thoughts; her father's death, Mr Tasman's investigation and her love for James. When he stopped the car he escorted her up to the door. She reached forward and kissed him on the cheek. 'I can't approve the investigation, but I just wish I'd had a grandad to love me, the way you love James.'

Alice was trying to decide between a floral and some stripes. She tapped out a costing and wished she was still eligible for the Tasman staff discount.

'Good afternoon! Can I be of some assistance, Miss Barrett?'

Ally looked up and smiled a greeting at Broderick Tasman. 'I'm being tempted. Both these designs offer possibilities.'

'Consider them over lunch. An old man would appreciate the company.'

She laughed. 'Thank you—I'm hungry! By the time I've lugged the sheeting...' she gestured to the assistant

who was unrolling metres of pastel poly-cotton for her
'. . . to and from the bus, I'll work off the calories.'

'Could I suggest our free delivery service?' Broderick
Tasman reached for the order book. 'I don't think you
realise just how heavy so many metres will be.'

'I had hoped to start work on it this afternoon.'

'At your home? Replacing the neighbourhood's linen
cupboards?' Broderick Tasman spoke to the assistant.
'Ring Delivery now. Tell them I request a code Z order.'
He swung back to Alice. 'It will be delivered within the
hour. My grandson would expect me to offer such a good
customer lunch.' They walked towards the coffee bar and
scrutinised the blackboard menu. 'You're aware that
James is in Nelson on business?'

'Yes, I drove him to the airport.' Ally glowed at the
memory.

'Yet you came in afterwards to buy fabric? I'm sure
James would have given you what you wanted.
Independence, privacy or both?'

They placed their orders and moved to a corner booth.

'I intend to make duvet covers and similar bedroom
and *en-suite* accessories for sale,' Ally explained. 'There's
a demand for a quality line at a lower price. At this stage
I'm just making up a few orders, but once these are
completed, I'd like to try my own design ideas.'

'Bravo! A young woman with initiative! But you
haven't discussed it with James. Why?'

'He works so hard already, I didn't think it was fair
to involve him.' She frowned, trying to be honest. 'I
think, too, I had some idea that if I could pull this off
without his help, I'd feel more confident—about myself,
my abilities. That I could make James happy, that I
wouldn't let him down. James could save me time,
hassles, and money, but if I can just ride out the start,
I should learn as I go.'

'Where are you intending to sell your work?'

'The market, I think. Tasman's would be the logical place, especially with the new speciality shop opening soon. But again it means involving James. Even if I contacted the buyer direct, the situation would be unfair. We often had lunch together when I was working here. It would place her in an embarrassing situation. Imagine if she had to say no!'

'Buyers for Tasman's turn down goods without a qualm.' Mr Tasman tapped his glass against the table. 'Establishing a small business isn't easy. Most fail. Usually there's a lack of capital and knowledge. You need a business partner.'

'Involve someone else?' Ally toyed with her salad.

'Yes. Someone with business expertise and money. I think you could make your ideas into a flourishing enterprise. You've found a gap in the market, you have the originality and capability of making the goods, and you work hard.'

'Wouldn't that be enough?' she asked.

'Possibly. But rather like trying to cook this fish pie without any experience or a recipe.'

'I see your point. But where am I going to find...?' She looked across at Broderick Tasman, who was smiling back at her. 'You'd help me? But why?'

'I was never averse to making a million here and there!' Broderick Tasman finished his fish pie and salad with an appreciative grin. 'If you won't ask James, then it could take you years of struggle without a qualified business partner. Pick the wrong person and you'll be ripped off. I don't want to see you getting involved with loans and usurious interest rates. If—and at this stage it's still subject to negotiation—if I put up the capital and expertise in production, retailing, warehousing and distribution, then I'd expect fifty per cent of the business. Once I see it established, I'll leave most of the organisation to you and the staff.'

'I'd like to consider your proposition.' Ally frowned. 'I don't want to seem ungrateful, I'm sure every word you've said is right. But it's very different from my concept!'

'Work out what you want, Ally. Set your own goals. Sort out ideas and put them on paper. Then give me a ring. But allow me to give you one tip. A manufacturer can't afford to pay retail for his bulk supplies. We buy sheeting from an Auckland importer and warehouseman. This is his address. You should make a visit there to see the range.' Broderick Tasman wrote the name and address on the back of one of his cards. 'Now, my dear Alice, I'd better get back to minding the store, or my grandson's not going to entrust it to me again!'

Ally walked with him back to the fabric counter, bought both the stripes and the floral, wrote a cheque, then walked out to the bus stop. Getting off at the park by her home, she sat under a bright green willow, mulling through the possibilities. Her original scheme might work, slowly building into a small business. It would give her confidence with James, teach her a little about his world of retailing. But if she failed? With Broderick Tasman's knowledge and backing, the enterprise was almost guaranteed. It would be wonderful to be able to help her family.

Her philosophic meanderings were broken by the arrival of a bus-load of teenage boys. They trooped on to the cricket area, and she recognised her brother's golden curls instantly. A chirpy wave told her he had noticed her presence, and she smiled back, deciding to watch the coaching practice. After warm-up exercises the boys split into teams, each having turns batting. Ally was no expert, but she was impressed with her brother's speed and skill when he fielded a stunning catch.

'Your brother, Jonathan Barrett?'

It was the coach who had asked her the question, and she nodded, watching Jonathan's progress.

'Thought so—same colour hair. Pity Jonathan has turned down the chance to tour Australia, he'd make the schoolboys' team.'

Ally looked at the man. She didn't want to give away the fact that Jonathan hadn't mentioned the proposed tour. 'The trip would be expensive?' she queried.

'We'll be subsidising it, but we expect the boys to raise half themselves. Some of them have jobs organised for the first couple of weeks of the holidays, and most families are willing to help. See if you can get Jonathan to change his mind. There's a month before the final team selection. They fly out after Christmas.'

Ally ached for her brother. He had said nothing because they couldn't afford such an experience. With a wave for Jonathan, she walked along to the cottage and checked the mailbox. The power bill and the telephone account were due but not welcome. As Ally climbed the steps to the house, she noticed the peeling paint on the weatherboards. Last year they had painted the roof; during the summer, the house would have to be sanded and painted. The click of the gate and her mother's footsteps as she inspected the mailbox, made Ally turn. Her mother stood, body slack, shoulders and neck drooped, weary. It seemed an effort for her to push her greying hair back from her face. In the unguarded moment, her mother looked worn, haggard and old.

Ally was shocked into action. She ran down the path and gave her mother a hug. To her horror, tears wobbled their way down her mother's face.

'Hey! Mothers aren't allowed to cry!'

'Ally! I've lost my job!'

Ally made her decision. 'That's great! You and Broderick Tasman and I are going into business. Third shares each! Come inside and we'll have a medicinal brandy to celebrate!' On the front porch a large parcel in Tasman's grey with burgundy stripe blocked their way. 'Our first delivery!' Ally pounced on it. 'Working together we can get through in half the time!'

Two weeks later, Ally waved goodbye to Broderick Tasman as he dropped her outside her home. Bulging suitcase in hand, she ran down the path to the front door.

'Ally! You're home!' Her mother hugged her. 'We missed you.'

'Auckland was great—I had a fantastic four days! Just wait till you see the stock I ordered! It's superb!'

'You kept to the budget?'

'Yes and no,' said Ally. 'I remembered to take down the codings for the other fabrics I liked so we can re-order by fax. There should be a courier delivery of laces arriving today. I could have spent the entire budget on laces alone! I've never seen anything like it.'

'How did you manage with Mr Tasman?'

'We had fun! You should have heard him bargain . . . he's a wily character, he saved us heaps. All the dealers made a fuss of him; we kept being taken out for lunch and dinners! I would have put on weight, only we were rushing around so fast, it hasn't been able to catch up with me! But here's the big news. Mr Tasman arranged a meeting with a visiting fabric manufacturer. I showed him my sketches and he pounced on my designs. In return for rights to two designs he's trading us special rates for six exclusive designs. That means we'll have six of our own fabrics next year! I would have been terrified by the size of the minimum order, but Mr Tasman trebled it and signed it without a murmur. He put a personal cheque into the company account to cover the payment. For about an hour we were wealthy! I have to decide on which designs to use, graph them and colour-swatch them within the month! Big executive!' Ally

laughed, golden curls alight, a halo of happiness. 'Imagine—our own designs!' She hugged her mother. 'It's
so exciting! How did you manage here? I felt quite bad
leaving you with half the first order to finish.'

'Somebody had to sew!' said her mother. 'I don't think
any of us realised quite what we were getting into! The
rep rang with his first report. In two days he's taken
enough orders to keep us flat-out for a month!
Everyone's wanting Alice's Cottage Crafts. The two
outworkers we hired are very good, but I hired another.
Katie has been sewing after school to help out; Jonathan
has learnt to fold and package, and he kept the records
straight of materials used and so on. Mrs Thwaites and
the twins popped in one day and she ended up helping
us out in the office. I've asked her to come back and
talk to you. We need someone there at least part-time.'

'That's wonderful! Mr Tasman was right—he said
we'd need more staff. Is there any mail for me? From
Australia?'

'No, but James rang from Sydney. The first time I
simply told him you weren't at home; the second time
he rang, Katie answered. She told him you were in
Auckland with his grandfather on a buying trip and
wouldn't be back until today.' Mrs Barrett shook her
head. 'I think you made a mistake not taking James into
your confidence about the partnership between us and
Broderick Tasman.'

'James will be home tomorrow. I'll explain it to him,
then.' Ally smiled at the thought. 'We've hardly seen
each other since the dinner party. He's been over in
Sydney for almost two weeks. So much has happened!'

'There's something else. A letter from your father's
attorney.'

Ally took the letter and skimmed the predictable first
paragraph, but the second riveted her attention. 'Dad
had sold a story to a film company? With all his ex-

penses and debts cleared the attorney expects to send you... Mum, it's a fortune!'

'Hardly that! But enough for a nest-egg and to freehold the house. There was only a small mortgage left, but I increased it to provide our stake in Alice's Cottage Crafts. Now I won't have to worry about instalments. Katie wants a large loom for her weaving, Jonathan has a cricket trip to Australia, but I'm not certain what to give you.'

'Save it for a wedding!'

'You're not serious! James is your first boyfriend! You hardly know him. Falling in love is the overture, marriage is the whole opera, and you want someone who'll be with you through the bad as well as the good scenes. Don't make my mistake, Alice. Give it time. In a few months you might feel quite differently.'

Ally hugged her mother. 'James loves me and I love him. What could possibly change that?'

CHAPTER TEN

BY CLOSING her eyes, Ally could see James smiling at her, telling her he loved and wanted her. His trip to his new shops had been necessary as he wanted to begin another mall changeover as soon as studies and finance would permit. Daily phone calls had been golden moments, his voice cherishing and warming. He had rung while she had been away, although she had laughingly told him he was not to phone so he could save the money for his mall! It was unfortunate that Katie had told him so much, but Ally admitted to herself that if James had been with her she would have been unable to keep the secret. Besides, she had gained confidence with the acceptance of her designs; the manufacturer had treated her as a professional.

Ally forced her dreams away. First she would give the presents she had bought for the family; then she would have to begin sewing. Work would deluge them—if she didn't begin soon, it would be easy to be swept away in the flood. Her mother and Broderick Tasman were counting on her ability and skills.

It was after midnight when she finished a bedroom and *en-suite* set, switched off her machine and wrote down her sewing time to the list of figures. While she worked, she had been listening for the telephone, but although she had calls from Anne and Chris James had not rung.

Katie had told him that she was due home, so why hadn't he called? An accident? Ambulances, screaming sirens, lights flashing, hospitals, surgeons in green... She pushed away the images; once he was home, she would ridicule her fears. Her pinpricked fingers smoothed the fabric into neat piles, and to distract herself, she began working out the machinist times for the set. Fatigue, kept at bay by the concentration on sewing, seeped through her when she began adding up. After miscalculating and smiling at the absurd result she decided to leave it for the new day.

Inspired by the thought, she checked the international flight timetable and saw that a plane should have just landed. Hope leaped in her heart that James could already be close. If she sat up for another half-hour, he would drive past on his way from the airport. If he saw the lights he would know she was waiting... Perhaps he would ring once he cleared Customs.

Her mouth curved into an enchanted smile as she imagined the rich, deep timbre of his voice, a sensual note... thrilling, melting, cosseting... Heart-lightened, she swayed ballerina-like, circling the room, dancing with James, the desk lamp transformed to a dazzling chandelier, the papered walls draped with pink satins, the music from the chipped radio their own private orchestra. Being in love and knowing you were loved was to dance on rainbows, surrounded by colour; shimmering gold, apricot, rose, madder-red, spinning into worlds of indigo-blue, purple and mauve.

Laughing at her fantasy, she collapsed back into the chair and, almost without being aware, she picked up her sketchbook and pencil and began roughing in two swirling ribbons that circled, entwined, then broke apart, only to be caught again and looped into smaller rings. Reaching for her colours, she made one strand blue for James; her strand had to be gold. The simplicity of the design appealed, but she could see other possibilities. Beginning again, she repeated the design, then covered the background with tiny dandelions, the long, toothed leaves reminiscent of acanthus, beloved of ancient artists and her own favourite Pre-Raphaelites. For the next page she repeated the basic design, setting in the golden flowers and the fourth page she backgrounded the design with clouds of dandelion clocks. Experimenting, she drew stripes, mixing, matching and miniaturising the patterns. On breaking the design into sections, she found she could do repeats of entwined gold and blue rings, ribbon scrolls, simple plants or repeats of flowers or seeds. If she needed a more complex pattern, she could combine different sections; leaves placed tip to stem and edged with ribbons formed a border pattern.

Exultant, she knew she had her exclusive fabric designs. In different colourways with light or dark backgrounds, she could mix and match with dozens of possibilities. There would be work graphing and detailing, but the idea was there. The only problem would be deciding which patterns were the best to send; the dandelion series could be a classic.

James would love it! She would make the first set up for their bedroom. The prospect caused the rainbow dancing dreams to begin again, and she pulled herself up with a jerk. It was almost two o'clock. James was not on the flight. Perhaps in the morning...

Despite the work piled up for her in the sewing-room and her mother's and Katie's additional help, the next day dragged the clock. Every phone call set her hopes high, only to be knocked down. When it was time to stop work, she was dispirited; the feeling of something wrong was heavy on her, a cloak of wet sand draped around her shoulders.

In front of the television she could not settle; instead like a caged panther she prowled the room, checked that the phone in the hall was working, went back and sat down for five minutes, then went out again to make sure she had put it back into the holder correctly. The family was irritated by her movements, she was disturbing their programme, so she slammed outside to the workroom and picked up the sketchpad. Looking at her dandelion design concentrated her thoughts and she began working on colour combinations.

The success of a saxe blue, grey and white combination helped occupy her, but she was clockwatching. The nine o'clock news confided the day's tragedies, but nothing connected with airline crashes or accidents. She switched off the radio, marched into her bedroom and picked up James's card on which he had scribbled his contact numbers. She rang the flat. The answerphone invited her to leave a message, so she tried James's private office line, but there was only the repetitive ringing. She fingered the buttons for the homestead numbers.

'James Tasman speaking.'

His voice sounded different. Ally was silent for a few seconds, wondering if the answerphone tape was distorting.

'James? Ally. You sound odd. At first I thought I was listening to the machine! When did you arrive? Are you all right? Have you caught a cold?' She waited for an answer, but the continued silence appalled. 'James? I missed you. When will I see you?'

'Never will be quite soon enough!'

Ally leaned against the wall. The wet-sand cloak was pressing on her, breathing was difficult. The joints and knuckles of her long fingers were almost the same colour as the ivory receiver. She tried to speak, but without air there was no sound.

'There's no point in prolonging this conversation. Our relationship is at an end.'

The click of the cut-off was definite. Ally replaced the phone, her movements stiff and unco-ordinated. Knees high, a jerky puppet, she staggered to her bedroom, then supported herself against the window-ledge. Her eyes focused without thought as she stared out of the window into the night. Across the road, she could see the uncurtained kitchen of the neighbour's, his television flickering greenly in one corner. Two sets of lights flashing along the road marked the brief passing of vehicles. Their red tail-lights faded. Wind rattled the stiff flax leaves. A cat yowled. Two dogs barked, then were silenced by a shrill, imperative whistle. Outside, everything was normal.

She looked round her bedroom. The patchwork duvet was creased where she had sat on it earlier; next to the bed stood the wide desk where she kept all her art materials, then the dressing table, her make-up in a row. Her curtained wardrobe bulged with the pressure of her clothes.

Inside, everything appeared the same. Yet nothing was.

'Our relationship is at an end.'

The words buzzed in her head. 'End. Our relationship. End. At an End.' Dimly, she was aware of falling, a void and a roar.

She came round slowly, struggling against the duvet threatening to bury her.

'Lie still a moment longer, Ally—you fainted. Katie, go and put the kettle on, make us all a cup of tea. Jonathan, get the heater. Bring it in here.'

An hour later, tucked into bed, and finally left alone, Ally had replayed the conversation and decided it had to be a cruel joke. Hadn't she thought the voice sounded odd? James could still be away. In an hour or two he might arrive at the door, his arms full of flowers. He loved her. Hadn't he told her so a million times?

The morning brought remembered reality. James had told her the relationship was ended. She had been Alice in Fantasyland. When he had left for Australia there had been no hint of any possible change. What had happened? Could he have met someone else? Realised he had made a mistake?

Wasn't she entitled to some explanation? Hadn't she feared she couldn't meet his expectations? What did she understand of his world of retailing? What did she have in common with him?

Their love was the only answer. If he no longer loved her was there any need to know the painful whys and how of his realisation?

Throughout the morning the question kept circling. She tried to cost a petticoat tablecloth with layers of lace, but seams which usually took less than a minute remained undone after half an hour. It was an effort to concentrate, and sometimes she would jerk, and realise she had been sitting at the machine, motionless. Finally she made up her mind. She would go to see James. Their love was worth a struggle. If something was wrong, there had to be an answer.

She dialled the private office line.

'Yes?'

The single word surprised her. 'James, it's Ally.'

'I'm in a meeting.'

Outrage and anguish mixed in her pain. 'Damn the meeting! James, I love you.' Disbelieving, she heard the intake of his breath and then the click as the line was cut. It took time to compose herself sufficiently to ring the store number and ask for his secretary. Over the past few weeks they had become friends.

'Ally? You want the boss? He's in a meeting, but it won't last much longer. He's been blowing heads off like coconuts this morning—Aussie must have been bad! At least, after he's talked to you, he'll be in a better mood.' There was a hint of a laugh. 'Let's see, he's got a gap at one for lunch. Why don't you take him out of the place for a while? We need the peace!'

Ally made up her mind. It was unlike James to be abrasive with staff. 'Write me in—officially. So James will see the appointment,' she said. If he was expecting her, he would know she had no intention of being fobbed off. Glancing at the hall clock, she realised there was little time for her to change and catch the bus to town. She threw off her jeans and pulled out a new dress from the wardrobe. With enforced care she slowed her movements as she eased on the matching sheer stockings.

Her make-up took five minutes. Her skin, naturally pale, seemed to be almost grey. Conscious that she had put on more make-up than usual, she checked her face in the mirror. Her brown eyes, troubled, looked back at her. Brushing her hair into free curls was the only solution to her golden frizz; there was no time to give it a more elaborate style. Lifting the dress into position, she slipped it over her shoulders, tugged it into line and zipped the front closed.

It was a dress she had made to wear when she was with James in private, its style revealing and enticing; a joke because he had teased her about her figure-hiding trousers and long-line tops. She grabbed up a jacket and flung it on, pushed her feet into unaccustomed high-heeled shoes and picked up her bag. There was just time to staccato down the path to the stop. In the bus, she reviewed her choice of dress, wishing she had worn the new business suit or her familiar, comforting jeans.

As she left the bus opposite Tasman's, she looked up to the jutting corner turret. James could be standing there watching her. The thought made her straighten her shoulders and toss her hair back.

Precisely on one o'clock she walked into the office.

'Ally! I tried to ring you. I'm sorry, but Mr Tasman is unable to see you.' The secretary's face showed her conflict.

'Unable or unwilling? Can you give me another appointment?'

'It would be no good. He was furious when he saw your name. He ordered me to cancel all his appointments this afternoon. I've also been instructed never to put through any calls from you.'

'I don't understand.' Ally's words were a whisper. 'I have a right to see him...'

'He's not here! He gave me the instructions and left.'

Ally was incredulous. It was out of character for James. His sense of responsibility was well defined. Cancelling appointments, being angry with staff, refusing to see her... Could he have suffered some type of breakdown? How long could someone work long hours without a backlash, either physical or mental? If he was suffering, she wanted to care for him, but first she had to see him and find the problem.

In the high-heeled shoes it took her fifteen minutes to walk to his flat. She remembered the previous time she had been there, just before he left for Australia. He had kissed her so lovingly that to think of it made her gasp with pain. Their relationship was at an end. Why? Could love be so ephemeral?

James's car was in the driveway. Her breathing became tugs at air. Her heart was jumping about, a frightened bird trapped in a cage. Slowing her steps, she enforced calm into her breathing, and the bird quietened.

The door was partially open as though James had walked in and been too weary to close it. Inside, she saw James by the fireplace, burning photographs. Shocked, she saw her own image curl and grey into ash.

'James!'

'You!' He spun round, his eyes blue fire. 'You dared come here?' He stood tall, facing her, the bunched chest muscles and the tightened forearm sinews signalling his rage.

Ally took an instinctive step back, intimidated, then locked her knees together, gripping courage. 'James, whatever the problem is, let me help! I love you!'

'Love? You?' His expression blazed contempt. 'You dirty the word! It's an excrescence in your mouth! With your pretence of innocence! I wanted the world for you. You were the perfect woman, a golden dream.' His voice was ice-sharded. 'But you were after the gold, not the dream. You set me up so perfectly, with your act of the virginal lily. I respected you, put you on top of a golden cloud, forcing myself to be patient.' He uttered a short laugh. 'Your acting ability is world class!'

'James, this is a nightmare! I haven't done anything!'

'Look at you! Tearful eyes, mouth all puckered in distress!' Again his self-mocking laugh. 'I'd swear you were innocent if I didn't know better!'

'Please, James. Just tell me what I'm supposed to have done.'

'Stop it!' He crashed his fist on the table. 'Lena flew over to tell me. You and the old man—my grandfather! It's obscene!'

Wide-eyed, Ally gazed at the man in front of her. He couldn't mean... The thought of sex with his grandfather was a ridiculous impossibility. But the look on James's face confirmed that he believed it. 'Your inference is disgusting! How could you think that about me? And your grandfather?' She was suffused with anger, but then she remembered the new business. 'Look, James, you've misunderstood. You've got it all wrong! It's a straightforward business partnership with my mother and your grandfather.'

'Yes, Lena told me you'd insisted on your mother being one of the partners too, just to make it look respectable. Your mother put in a token amount, a fraction of what my grandfather paid for his rights in the so-called deal! He made sure of his claim in the document. Bedroom products to be supplied by Alice's Cottage Crafts!'

'You're wrong! I was going to tell you about it!'

'Others told me! I heard about your Auckland jaunt from different sources; how the old man was accompanied by a gorgeous golden chick. Lena had hoped to spare me that, but Katie confirmed it.'

He moved forward, trapping her against the wall. 'You're nothing but a very expensive prostitute!'

Frozen, she felt him strip off her sleeveless jacket.

'I see you've changed your dress style.' His mouth twisted. 'This is the real you. A woman confident of her sexual prowess.' His hands travelled over the close-fitting garment, exploring her shape.

She flinched. 'Stop it!' Her voice was a whisper of misery.

'Why? You didn't stop at the first success!' He rammed his hands in his pockets as though to physically separate them from her body. 'Did you seriously think I'd stand by and watch you disinherit my mother, my brother and sister?'

'What . . . ?'

'Spare me the innocent routine—it's boring! Lena's always been close to our family. As she said, she'd rather forget her professional ethics than risk you disinheriting my family. She was appalled when Grandad asked her for up-to-date valuations on all his domestic property, but when he asked for possible ways to break the trusts he set up for my family, it was too much. He told her he wants to liquidate some of his assets and he wants a new will prepared,' James paused for effect, 'because he wants to show his affection for little Alice!'

'No! I like, admire and respect your grandfather. He's never——'

'You're too greedy—planning to sell the homestead! You'd throw my mother out of her home! And my sister and brother! Look at these photo-copies! That's my grandfather's signature on the authorisations.' James thrust some papers under her nose. 'See, there and there!'

'Stop it! I can't...' The smell of the treated paper made her nauseous. 'I never thought you could be cruel.'

'Me? You are the expert. Cruelty was destroying the bond between my grandfather and me. You've turned him into an old goat, salivating with lust. You must be magnificent in bed!'

Ally's heart pounded into double time as she realised his intent. He reached out and tugged at the zip at her shoulder, and instinctively she clutched at it, stopping his action.

'Your shape appears superb,' he drawled. 'But I'd like an inspection before I decide to buy five minutes. That should be long enough.'

It was the ultimate insult. Ally looked at the man in front of her, her own anger dying when she saw the hate, corrosive as acid, eating at him. He was destroying himself with jealousy, wounded pride and rage, the intensity an outpouring of the dream they had shared. His ideal smashed, he was becoming embittered, cynical, a user rather than a giver, a grotesque shadow of the gentle man she loved. Compassion helped her understand. So many facts pointed to her guilt. How could she prove innocence when nothing had happened?

She swallowed. There was a way. Finding her a virgin would tell him he had been wrong. It would give them a chance to find their love.

'I would need to be protected.' Her words were raw.

'I wouldn't think of having sex without a condom.'

His hand reached again for her zip and began to reveal her body. She had wanted the moment to be so full of love, a time to explore and share each other completely... In despair she hung her head, not wanting to see the anger in his eyes. Her hair fell obediently forward, protecting her as the dress fell to the floor. When he removed her bra, she shut her eyes. She wanted to scream at him, 'No! Not like this!'

She bit her tongue in the effort to keep silent as he slid down her knickers and tights, the elastic reluctant to leave her skin. Her abdomen spasmed as his hands touched. Her whole body quivered.

'I knew you'd be beautiful,' the comment was dragged from him. 'Your skin is smooth, like sunwarmed marble.' He lifted her hair back on to her shoulders, but she kept her head bent. She did not want him to see the tears poised to drip from her eyes.

'You prefer to keep your eyes closed?'

She nodded, unable to speak.

'So you can't see your lovers?' His voice was rough.

'Please, James...' Her heart was doing its frightened bird leaps and her breathing was fast and shallow. The shivering of her body she could not control.

'I'd prefer a slightly more welcoming position. The virginal violet might do a lot for the ego of an old man, but it doesn't appeal to me!'

Her whole being rebelled. James could think her guilty. He wanted to punish her, but she was allowing him to degrade her.

'That's enough, James. I'm not going through with this...' As she spoke she grabbed up her panties, pulling them into place. She was confident with her decision. Her bra took a moment to fit and fasten. James, she noted, had remained still, his eyes blue ice, only his sensuous lips twisted into a grimace.

'I never had any intention of touching you! Only a fool swims in muddy waters.' He scooped up her dress and threw it towards her. 'Now I'll tell you my terms. If you make my grandfather happy, I've no quibbles over him paying you a small wage through your so-called partnership, but I insist on discretion. Not one word is to reach the rest of the family. You can keep what my grandfather has already given you. If I hear that my grandfather intends gifting you any property or money, or making you a major beneficiary in his will, I'll take action.'

Ally cringed at the loathing in his eyes.

'One thing more. If you're at my grandfather's when I call, I'll expect you to keep out of my sight. You will turn down any invitations to the homestead. I don't ever wish to see you again. Don't you ever forget, I protect my own!'

She eased on her dress, zipped it into position, then stood, straight and proud, beyond anger. 'One day you'll learn the truth, James. I was prepared to give you the proof—my virginity.' She slipped on her jacket and high heels and walked out of the door.

CHAPTER ELEVEN

ALLY rubbed the back of her neck, where a large tension knot had formed. The dimpled metal on her index finger scraped, a thimble seemed to have become an extension of her hand. Yawning, she stretched, but the slither of the fabric off her knee snapped her back to concentration. Grabbing the duvet cover she had been hand finishing, she folded it and put it aside. The clock showed midnight. Another day was over. She could go to bed and if she was lucky, she would fall asleep. It had been almost six weeks since the scene with James.

With stiffened muscles from sitting too long, Ally eased herself off the chair and walked to the workroom door. Switching off the power, she padlocked the door after her, then walked the few steps along the path to the back porch. The night air revived her and she was wide awake when she slipped into her bedroom. She took the day's tally from the print-out in her pocket and transferred it to the book she kept on her desk. Each day she was whittling away at the sum the company owed James's grandfather, but at times she felt like a mouse faced with nibbling her way through a bale of wool. If she could have, she would have repaid Mr Tasman's investment. James's remembered taunts punishing her like a goad, she had no choice but to carry on. The long hours were a form of numbing relief; while she was working, the pain of the last scene with James kept in the distance.

She re-read the figures and knew that Broderick Tasman would be happy with the week's results. Again they had surpassed the projected figures. Her mother's and her own new knowledge of bookkeeping and computing was a result of tutelage Mr Tasman had arranged. The lessons had not been easy for Ally, but her mother showed remarkable aptitude for accounting and distribution. Mrs Thwaites, employed in the office while the twins were at kindergarten, had helped Ally understand.

Ally closed the book and, like a sleepwalker, undressed, showered and crawled into bed. Tears began dripping from her eyes, like taps with worn washers. She reached over for the tissues by the side of the bed and two tears plopped on to the polished wooden floor. Hadn't another Alice been at risk of drowning from her own pool of tears? Blowing her nose, she knew it was better to think of work. Thoughts of James only meant another sleepless night.

The selling agent Broderick Tasman had recommended had been helpful, reporting excellent sales. The man had been surprised by her instruction not to offer any products to the stores owned by James Tasman, but the rule remained. James could crawl to her before she would let him stock her wares. As far as she was concerned, personality did come into business! She tried to imagine an abject James, his hands held out pleadingly, but it didn't work. He stood, laughing, throwing dandelions at her.

She turned over again, the one blanket too hot. Why did he continue to haunt her? A day earlier she had been waiting at the bus stop and James had crossed the street. Her heart had pounded and her brain functioned in slow time. He'd looked just the same, the ruggedly handsome physique, the thick, well cut dark hair, the blue eyes lit in a smile as he acknowledged one of the staff. As though he had sensed her presence, he had looked in her direction, and their glances met. Hate had sparked in his eyes, his regard trampled her, his tan skin greyed. Then he had deliberately walked away. She shivered, and pulled the blanket back up again as though it could protect her.

With an effort to switch her thought pattern she recalled the twins. Earlier in the afternoon they had visited, and she relaxed, remembering their chuckles when they found the glove puppets she had made from a few scraps. A smile crept across her face. Greer and Geoffrey had enjoyed the toys, and their imagination as they redressed the puppets had been fun. She wondered if she should include rag dolls or glove puppets in with the children's bedroom sets. Tomorrow she would do a costing. Or rather today...

At half-past six the bedside alarm woke her. By seven she was working again, her machine buzzing like a maddened bee. It was ten o'clock when Broderick Tasman asked to enter the workroom. She felt his shrewd regard.

'My dear Alice, I'm rather anxious about you.' He had smiled to soften the words. 'You're looking more like a dandelion that's been sprayed with herbicide than the colourful young woman my grandson brought to see me. You're turning into a workaholic. Take some time off—you need a break.'

'No, thank you, Mr Tasman, I'm fine.' Her voice wobbled, betraying her. To cover herself she grabbed the first item in a pile of handsewing, threading the needle expertly.

'I know you and my grandson decided to break up, but I believe the two of you have made a mistake. You're miserable and as for James...I've not seen him! He put the assistant manager in charge here temporarily, and he went back to Sydney to work on the mall ideas. One of my old friends there told me James is like a prowling, snarling tiger. He flew home two days ago, but unfortunately I was in Auckland and he went back to Sydney just before I arrived home. If it weren't so ridiculous I'd think he was trying to avoid me! On the phone he's barely civil, and sometimes I think even that's an effort. I've tried asking him about you and he cut the connection. Obviously it's too painful for him to be able to discuss it. If I knew what went wrong, perhaps I could help untangle it.'

Ally looked at the old man and saw the new lines of sadness around his mouth. He was being hurt, and he had done nothing wrong. Yet she couldn't tell Broderick Tasman the unpalatable truth.

'I'm afraid it's not so simple. I made a minor mistake, a matter I should have discussed with James. It was misinterpreted by someone else. James was convinced I had an interest in your money and property. There was a...an unpleasant scene. Please, Mr Tasman, I can't say any more.'

Broderick Tasman frowned. 'But there is more, isn't there? James knows you're not materialistic, it was one of the first things he told me about you.' He paused. 'So for him to believe otherwise, there must have been evidence.'

'I'm sorry, Mr Tasman,' she could feel the sharp tears pricking at the back of her eyes, 'I have to finish this casing.'

'Love makes us vulnerable,' he sighed, and patted her shoulder. 'You need help, I believe. Or at least time to sort things out and find some peace. What about Fiji? Golden sand, warm water and coconut palms. You'd enjoy it. I'd be happy to pay for you and a friend...'

'No! No—I can't! You've already given me too much!' She was in a panic at the thought of James finding out about the offer. Belatedly, she realised she was overreacting. 'I'm sorry, that wasn't very gracious of me. I owe you so much already. I'd like to be able to pay you back the extra money as quickly as possible. I've put aside most of my wages, but it's going to take a long time . . . as a matter of fact, while you were away, I went to see several bank loan officers to see if I could borrow the amount, but they refused. Without security, I'm not an acceptable risk. Naturally I didn't mention your name.' She looked sadly at the man who reminded her so much of James. 'It would have helped my pride to have been able to repay you.'

'You're worried by the money? Don't be! I've a little more foresight and knowledge of you than those bank managers! My Alice would have approved of you. She always said I had an instinctive ability to pick the winners in the stock. And I was right!' Mr Tasman produced a letter from his briefcase. 'The fabric manufacturer. First, he and his key staff are so impressed with the designs you sent, they're going to give us a priority run.'

'Does that mean we'll have the exclusive designs soon?'

'Yes—and more! This man who deals in fabric all day, every day, believes the dandelion series will be a hit. I know manufacturers. He's recognised your ability and he knows your backing. He's suggested we negotiate a further contract; he wants to be our exclusive supplier for your designs on a long-term basis, and the terms he's offered appear very much in our favour.' Mr Tasman handed her the letter. 'Congratulations! I'll consult a couple of people I respect and do some homework on the deal before the next board meeting.'

'So long as it's the same percale and thread count...it looks great. He's talking five years with a right of renewal!' Ally skimmed the pages. 'He's very flattering about my designs.'

'If you'd walked into a bank with that paper in your hand you would have been given your loan! Ally, you're going to have more money than you know what to do with! With your ideas and practical ability the market will start knocking at your door! I can see factories around the world. Alice's Cottage Crafts selling in

Sydney, London, Rome, Tokyo, Toronto, Paris, New York!'

'You have a great imagination!'

'I'm a wily old bird! Together with your mother, we're a great team, but the team will collapse if the designer can't do her work. It's your originality, Alice, which is at the centre, so, in order to protect our investment, I'm ordering you to take at least a week off. Now finish that casing and then leave. If you won't let me pay for a holiday, then accept the loan of the beach house for a week or two. You'll be doing me a favour by occupying it, otherwise, with James away, it will be empty until the school holidays.'

Ally lay on the white sand of the beach, its sunwarmed heat pleasant on her skin. The beach was deserted and the isolation soothed. Broderick Tasman had been right, she had needed time to face her loss, time to let the idle thoughts cleanse and heal, time to look at the life ahead. She had been close to exhaustion. The simplicity and comfort of the beach cottage appealed, its windows looking over the sea, and on one side to the hill and bush she had painted on the mural.

Inevitably, her thoughts turned to James. After much anger, comprehension and compassion had helped her to understand his emotions. At times she could almost feel his rage.

She had been on her own five days, five days during which she had lain in bed, slept when she could, sun-baked cautiously, ate when she wanted, walked in the hills and just sat and watched the sunset light the sea. There had been times of being lonely, but the rare indulgence of being able to do as she liked had compensated.

The swish forward and swirl back of the waves formed a gentle, repetitive pattern that relaxed. The early summer day had been unseasonably hot, a temptation to swim, but a toe-dunking trial had convinced her that the sea still had to warm. Swimming alone in cold water was dangerous and foolhardy—common sense told her that. As it had told her that falling in love with a man like James Tasman was stupid, illogical. She had known it from the beginning.

So why did it all hurt so much? And what was she going to do to help Mr Tasman? He had lost his wife and his only child and now his grandson. During the trip to Auckland, Ally had found Mr Tasman open about his apathy to the business after his wife's death. He blamed himself for the lack of training he had given his son, for not realising that the business was failing with the changing times, and admitted that after his son's death it was only on James's insistence that he had taken control again. Working with James had renewed his flair and his old ability to strike bargains. It was James who had persuaded him that new retailing techniques had to be practised, including designing the new mall out of the old department store. For James, Broderick Tasman had made the effort. Ally's eyes showed sadness as she remembered the love so natural between the pair. Lena had been destructive and savage in her target.

'It's just not fair!' Ally threw a shell towards the sea with her cry of despair and anger. 'What am I going to do?'

A seagull cawed mockingly.

Absently she stroked some more sunblock on her legs. The smell of it permeated summer. Using a towel to protect her hair, she lay back on the sunwarmed sand and closed her eyes, searching for inspiration. If she went to Lena and promised to stay out of James's life, would Lena admit to James how the documents had been twisted and mixed? She shook her head, answering her own question. Lena would know such an admission would mean the loss of James's friendship as well as the Tasman account.

Ally sighed and rolled over. In the movies it was all so easy—someone used a tape recording to trap the guilty one into providing evidence. Lena would be more than capable of defensive action, Ally guessed. It was too late ever to salvage her love for James, but for his grandfather's sake she had to think of something.

The umbrella she had set up earlier was shading her back and the sudden loss of warmth chilled. Surprised, she rolled over again and reached out to adjust it.

'Allow me!'

He was backlighted by the sun, his face in shadow. As if she was hallucinating, she scrunched up the skin round her eyes and shook her head. He was still there, his hands firm on the umbrella pole as he angled it.

'James!' Her voice was a croak. She forced courage back into her body. Hadn't James Tasman taught her the value of her own dignity? She sat up. 'If you want the cottage, I'll leave immediately.'

He moved to stand in front of her. 'I came to see you. To apologise.'

A thousand regrets flickered in her mind.

'I'm sorry, Ally.'

Imagination had painted more. Fanfares of triumph, bucketloads of flowers. James eating dust. Yet the simplicity made his sincerity strong.

'I regret the charges I made that you were having sex with my grandfather. For money.'

The words were shame-stiff. Ally saw how he forced himself to look at her, saying the words as though he had rehearsed them. A sense of justice had made him face her, but at the end, his voice withered.

'I'm sorry. I know I hurt you.' His formality crumbled. He turned, looking out to sea, his knuckles white as he scrabbled together his control.

Ally looked at James; under a deeper tan, new sorrow lines were etched on his face. 'What made you change your mind?'

'Grandad sent me a courier package. He wrote asking for my opinion on a contract and said he'd already sent it on to a specialist in contract law. He set out the figures in his letter, so I was intrigued by the length and size of the deal before I even opened the contract. When I saw the name Alice's Cottage Crafts as the company involved, with the other being an reputable fabric manufacturer, I was furious. I couldn't believe that Grandad would be so insensitive as to ask me to have anything to do with your partnership. I was volcanic for an hour; I didn't even want to think about it, but figures that didn't make sense keep flitting through my brain like mosquitoes. Apart from that, I wondered why Grandad would want to get involved in such complications, when Lena had said the partnership was just a discreet way to pay you. I was forced to go back and read the contract, and that in turn made me examine the complete printout and tax record Grandad had enclosed.'

'Your grandad sent you those details?' Ally stood up, indignant. 'You're the last person I would have allowed . . .' She faltered, honesty attacking her. 'I remember giving permission for Mr Tasman to show them to an expert but I didn't expect you!'

'You're upset, Ally, but I think Grandad had an ulterior motive. Those papers forced me to acknowledge that a genuine business existed.' James ran his left hand through his hair. 'I had difficulty in thinking about you. It was easier to hate you. But I kept dreaming about you, only to wake up to the nightmare. I was afraid of my own rage. To face those figures, I had to lecture myself that I had to know what was going on, to protect my family.'

Under his scrutiny she looked away, brushing off the grains of sand which had dried on her.

'The receipts you'd collected from the guesthouse in Auckland really shook me. Grandad had stayed at his apartment, but there were taxi chits showing where and when he picked you up each day and the addresses you visited and where he dropped you off each evening. I recognised the addresses; fabric suppliers, lace importers. Further down, there were the corresponding dockets for goods purchased. Then there were the increasing staff lists and their tax numbers, even Mrs Thwaites working for you part-time in the office.'

'So you decided there was a little business,' Ally said waspishly.

'Yes—one with immense potential. The contract proves it. But until I got down to the wages breakdown, I believed the term sleeping partner was a more appropriate way to describe my grandfather's interest.' He turned away for a moment, looking at the sea. 'But your wages made me reconsider. Apart from a small amount which would barely feed you, all your wages, after tax, are going back to my grandfather. In addition, a smaller portion of your mother's wage also goes to his account. It's towards repayment of a sum Grandad paid to the fabric manufacturer who's making up your own designs. The same one in the contract.' James turned back to her. 'If you'd been the gold-digger I accused you of being, you wouldn't have beggared yourself repaying it. The woman who could persuade my grandfather to sell my home and his other domestic property wouldn't have been troubled about such a loan.' Mechanically, he had been kicking at a buried stick. It flew free, scattering sand.

'Ally, I didn't have the answer. There were too many pieces to a jigsaw, I kept remembering your face when

I'd accused you, the horror and anger, then your capitulation.' His voice broke. 'Ally, please don't cry. I can't…'

'I'm not!' She sniffed and bent down to pick up her sarong, brushing her arm against her eyes, to swiftly wipe the tears. Sand stung her eyes, a grain sticking barbarously sharp. James putting his arms around her to hold her hands was too much. 'Don't you touch me!'

'Wait! Be still!' He released her, then took out a white handkerchief, shaking it ostentatiously. 'Truce? If you try to remove that sand, you'll make it worse.'

She barely felt the touch of the cloth at the corner of her eye, but the relief of the irritation was immediate. He brushed the rest of the sand off as he mopped her face.

'Blow!'

She blew, then grabbed the handkerchief. Some things she could do better herself; in fact, she didn't need James Tasman at all! Feelings tumbling over one another, she tried to stop her body from trembling. She knotted the sarong around her and sat down, suddenly too exhausted to stand. When James sat down beside her she knew sitting had been a mistake. She fought for an appearance of calm. 'How do you explain Lena's evidence?'

'It was all in the rest of the courier package. Grandad said that results on the mall at home had exceeded expectation and staff morale was champagne. He had hoped to discuss it with me, but since he hadn't seen me he'd wanted me to know he planned to make all Tasman stores into malls. He set out his options. Course one called for the mall changeovers to be completed, within twelve months. With the number of shops in the Tasman chain that option meant big money—millions. To raise it he would need to borrow heavily, and he would have been forced to sell most of his domestic property and mortgage even the homestead. He'd authorised Lena to arrange valuations, and to check that a receiver couldn't break the family trusts, as the option risked bankruptcy. Naturally it meant rearranging his will. Course two involved changing as money became available, over a fifteen-year period. He realised that was too slow. Course three is a compromise. He'll go ahead with the malls, but over a five-to six-year period. He intends to sell some property, like his Auckland and Wellington apartments, to raise extra cash, so he doesn't have to mortgage the homestead. Profit flows from the first, completed malls will provide the cash for the last stage.'

'So, suddenly, I'm not the wicked witch who was going to banish your mother from her home!'

'Ouch!' The blue eyes were rueful. 'As I read the letter I could see how Lena had manipulated the documents. Before I left for Sydney, I'd told her that I intended to marry you as soon as I returned. It never occurred to me that Lena had planned to marry me! She didn't love me, she just thought I'd be suitable—and eventually rich! Two days later Grandad walked in and gave her the authorisations, outlining his three options. Lena deliberately misused those documents. I called in on her, on the way back from the airport this afternoon. I demanded her resignation from the law firm and advised her to leave the country permanently, if she didn't want me to hand over the details to the Law Society. She wrote out her resignation and took it in to the senior partner, her excuse being that she wants to pursue her music in Europe.

'I went to your home, but your mother wasn't there. Instead I saw Mrs Thwaites. She's quite a champion of yours! And she refused to tell me where you were or when you'd be back. On the way out I was ambushed by the twins, and Greer gave me a shell. I went to see Grandad. When he hugged me, I knew that I'd been a fool, driven by jealousy and rage. I told him I was looking for you, but he wouldn't tell me where you were.

He said I'd caused you great unhappiness, that you'd needed a break as you'd been working fourteen-and sixteen-hours days...it was quite a lecture. I only took it from him because I could see he was enjoying himself. He sent me those papers because he wanted to get us back together. Apparently you'd protected me when he began asking questions.'

'I did it for him. He loves you!' Ally finished abruptly, annoyed that she was explaining anything to James Tasman. He didn't deserve explanations!

'He refused to tell me where you were. He said he'd have to check with you first.'

'So how did you find me?'

'Greer's shell. I'd put it on the passenger car seat. I remembered how often I'd come here when decisions had to be made, especially at this time of the year, when it's peaceful. I thought it was worth a try. Greer brought us together—the shell was an omen.' He paused and looked at her. 'Darling dandelion, I know I hurt you. Forgive me?'

Ally, eyes down, remembered. Sand glistened like gold dust on her legs. She lifted her head and gazed at the curve of the beach; the shoreline scalloped with faint white lace, the wave trails running from and towards the sea, a picture-postcard scene.

'I accept your apology. And your explanation. Now you can leave.'

'Alice?'

Her formal name. Why was he sitting there? Waiting for what?

She risked a glance. It was a mistake. His blue eyes had always spoken for him.

'Ally!'

She shook her head and decided formality protected her. 'Please go. At least now, perhaps we can accept what happened. We can be free of each other and able to form new relationships.'

'You know that isn't possible. I love you. You're the only woman I've ever loved.'

'You love me?' His words broke the zip on the bulging bag of emotions she had struggled to control. She stood up, shouting as she ran away. 'How can you say that?' Her movement was slowed by the ankle-deep loose sands and the first rocks. 'Damn you, James Tasman!'

'Ally, it was what I didn't do that proves it!'

He was beside her as she began climbing up the rocks, keeping pace as she scrambled on to the hill. The grass was easier to run on. She was shaking, furious with herself for revealing her vulnerability. Deciding on the haven of the bush, she ran towards it, but he was already ahead of her. Shocked, she realised he was stooping to pick some wild yellow flowers. Dandelions! Panting, trembling, she stood at bay.

'Ally, I'd desired you so much, I'd planned our love-making in exquisite detail. Somehow, when I thought you'd betrayed us, all that emotion channelled into fury. I was almost mad with rage when I saw you, pretending innocence, as I thought.'

She felt sick, remembering.

'I didn't physically harm you, because your distress, your feelings, conquered my black temper. Despite my rage, you held the gentle power of love. When I lifted your hair back, I saw your eyelashes were tipped with your tears, and I hated myself. You have to forgive me, Ally.' He presented the dandelions.

'No!' Her protest was loud. She already remembered another bouquet, when he had been patient and under-standing and she had admitted her fear and her love. She looked at him. His blue eyes revealed his regret. 'You're not being fair!' She flung the dandelions back.

'Because you can't remain angry with me? You understand me, therefore you can't hate me? And you're afraid? Afraid you're still attracted to me? Afraid because you don't want to love me.'

It was the truth, but she remained silent, clenching and unclenching her fists to keep her body from trembling.

'I know I've hurt you, Ally.' He took her hands, stopping her frantic fingers. 'I'm not sure if I can make it up to you. Perhaps a lifetime won't be enough. But I intend to try.' He lifted her hands and kissed first one, then the other.

The touch of his lips on her skin threatened her. Ally bent her head and the curtain of her hair swung forward, covering her chaos.

'No, don't hide from me. There's too much pain.'

Surprised by the agony in his tone, she looked up at him and saw the grief lines deepen on his face. Her instinctive gesture had slashed open his feelings. She had suffered, but thinking about her had tormented him. What had he said about the gentle power of love? What did she really want?

To satisfy her pride? To hurt him more? Or to admit her own need and love as she had before? She saw the blue flame leap as she moved towards him and leaned forward, nestling herself against his, feeling the shudders of his body, her arms enfolding him. For a time they stood, arms holding each other, forgiving, understanding.

'Dandelion!'

It was a murmur of love tickling against her ear. She felt his breath blow the strands of hair away and desire engulfed her. Reaching up, she knew he was waiting for her response, and she riffled her fingers through his thick, soft hair, then, in slow motion, circled her left ring fingertip round his right ear. She saw the smile in his eyes as he repeated her gesture, stranding her long curls, touching her earlobes, then slipping his hands to hold her face in his firm, sensitive fingers. His kiss was a feather, then a bird's wingbeat against the sky. Repeating it, he kissed her a dozen times, each time deepening the movement until she was flying with him, soaring and dipping and wheeling in exultation.

'Darling dandelion! You intoxicate me!' With a groan, he kissed her possessively, his hands tightening to hold her even more closely. 'Dandelion wine!' He smiled at her. 'You wanted to say something?' His lips tantalised her mouth, effectively stopping her speech. 'If it's to tell me you love me, I know.'

Her full lips shaped a kiss. He was right, of course. Other feelings had swarmed rebelliously, but she had tossed them away in her forgiveness. No one else had caused a shadow of the emotion she felt for James. With him she was beautiful; a sensual, warm, passionate woman, complete. Without him—— She shivered.

Work. Would James understand? 'I do love you. But I have other responsibilities. People relying on me—your grandfather, my mother, our staff—I won't throw away their trust. The business is exciting, but I'm ready to experiment further. I'd like to set up more of a co-operative venture, already I've done some homework on the staff share plan...' She broke off, hearing his chuckle.

'You're marrying a Tasman, so I can hardly protest. In fact, our businesses could be complementary. Each one of the Tasman stores could have an Alice's Cottage Craft boutique.'

'I'll consider the idea!' she teased, 'and raise it at the board meeting. I don't think we'll be big enough to support that for about three years. We're still developing our lines.'

'That gives me time to add to our Australian chain. The mall rebuilding programme will be over and we'll have capital to invest. Perhaps by then we might take a lengthy period of time off, to see the world together. We can give some time to saving the rainforests or the whales or the ozone layer... and think of starting our family, my kaleidoscope madonna. I know you love children, but do you want them, if it means interrupting your career?'

'Being a designing woman is the interlude, not my career!' Ally smiled. 'I knew what I was doing when I trained as a nanny! Of course I want children! I'll hand over my share of Alice's Cottage Crafts to someone else, possibly Katie. Maybe I'll work one or two afternoons a week as a designer. I want time to be with you...' Her voice tailed off as the warmth of his caress made her breathless. James was blowing away the last sand crystals which had cloaked on her skin.

'Forever and ever, my darling Alice.' His kiss was the touch of a dandelion parachute.

Accept 4 FREE Romances and 2 FREE gifts

FROM READER SERVICE

Here's an irresistible invitation from Mills & Boon. Please accept our offer of 4 FREE Romances, a CUDDLY TEDDY and a special MYSTERY GIFT!

Then, if you choose, go on to enjoy 6 captivating Romances every month for just £1.80 each, postage and packing FREE. Plus our FREE Newsletter with author news, competitions and much more.

**Send the coupon below to:
Mills & Boon Reader Service,
FREEPOST, PO Box 236,
Croydon, Surrey CR9 9EL.**

- - - NO STAMP REQUIRED - - -

Yes! Please rush me 4 FREE Romances and 2 FREE gifts! Please also reserve me a Reader Service subscription. If I decide to subscribe I can look forward to receiving 6 brand new Romances for just £10.80 each month, post and packing FREE. If I decide not to subscribe I shall write to you within 10 days - I can keep the free books and gifts whatever I choose. I may cancel or suspend my subscription at any time. I am over 18 years of age.

Ms/Mrs/Miss/Mr _____ EP55R

Address _____

_____

Postcode _____ Signature _____

mps MAILING PREFERENCE SERVICE

ESCAPE INTO ANOTHER WORLD...

...With Temptation Dreamscape Romances

Two worlds collide in 3 very special Temptation titles, guaranteed to sweep you to the very edge of reality.

The timeless mysteries of reincarnation, telepathy and earthbound spirits clash with the modern lives and passions of ordinary men and women.

Available November 1993   Price £5.55

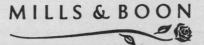

Next Month's Romances

Each month you can choose from a wide variety of romance with Mills & Boon. Below are the new titles to look out for next month, why not ask either Mills & Boon Reader Service or your Newsagent to reserve you a copy of the titles you want to buy — just tick the titles you would like and either post to Reader Service or take it to any Newsagent and ask them to order your books.

Please save me the following titles:	Please tick	√
DAWN SONG	Sara Craven	
FALLING IN LOVE	Charlotte Lamb	
MISTRESS OF DECEPTION	Miranda Lee	
POWERFUL STRANGER	Patricia Wilson	
SAVAGE DESTINY	Amanda Browning	
WEST OF BOHEMIA	Jessica Steele	
A HEARTLESS MARRIAGE	Helen Brooks	
ROSES IN THE NIGHT	Kay Gregory	
LADY BE MINE	Catherine Spencer	
SICILIAN SPRING	Sally Wentworth	
A SCANDALOUS AFFAIR	Stephanie Howard	
FLIGHT OF FANTASY	Valerie Parv	
RISK TO LOVE	Lynn Jacobs	
DARK DECEIVER	Alex Ryder	
SONG OF THE LORELEI	Lucy Gordon	
A TASTE OF HEAVEN	Carol Grace	

If you would like to order these books in addition to your regular subscription from Mills & Boon Reader Service please send £1.80 per title to: Mills & Boon Reader Service, Freepost, P.O. Box 236, Croydon, Surrey, CR9 9EL, quote your Subscriber No:.................................... (If applicable) and complete the name and address details below. Alternatively, these books are available from many local Newsagents including W.H.Smith, J.Menzies, Martins and other paperback stockists from 3 December 1993.

Name:..

Address:..

......................................Post Code:........................

To Retailer: If you would like to stock M&B books please contact your regular book/magazine wholesaler for details.

You may be mailed with offers from other reputable companies as a result of this application. If you would rather not take advantage of these opportunities please tick box ☐